HIS
UNFORGETTABLE
FIANCÉE

HIS UNFORGETTABLE FIANCÉE

BY

TERESA CARPENTER

First published in Great Britain 2015
by Mills & Boon, an imprint of Harlequin (UK) Limited,
Large Print edition 2015
Eton House, 18-24 Paradise Road,
Richmond, Surrey, TW9 1SR

© 2015 Teresa Carpenter

ISBN: 978-0-263-25711-3

Harlequin (UK) Limited's policy is to use papers that are natural, renewable and recyclable products and made from wood grown in sustainable forests. The logging and manufacturing processes conform to the legal environmental regulations of the country of origin.

Printed and bound in Great Britain
by CPI Antony Rowe, Chippenham, Wiltshire

This book is dedicated to
Patty, Maria and the gang at the Grab & Go
on 6th Street, downtown San Diego.
Much of my books are written during lunch.
Thank you for your service and your patience.
And for not throwing me out
when I'm the last one there.

CHAPTER ONE

"G. DELANEY, YOU look beautiful tonight." Chet Crowder slurred the compliment.

Sheriff Grace Delaney glanced down at her khaki uniform, thought of her black cap of hair slicked back for convenience and her lack of makeup beyond a swipe of mascara and a touch of lip gloss, and figured if she needed any further evidence of Chet's intoxication she had proof of it in that comment.

"Is it midnight yet?" the eighty-year-old demanded. "I get a kiss at midnight." The words barely left his mouth when he bent over and puked all over the slick concrete floor.

"It's against procedures to kiss the prisoners." Grace cited policy as she nimbly avoided the deluge, stepping around the mess to escort him to the middle cell.

"But it's New Year's Eve," Chet protested with a burp. "You can make an ex-exception for New Year's Eve."

He didn't have to tell her it was New Year's Eve. Not even eleven o'clock and they already had three D and Ds—drunk and disorderly. Business as usual for the holiday. But not much longer for her. In a little over an hour she'd be handing over her gun and shield, her interim assignment as sheriff at an end.

"Rules are made for a reason," she stated. Her father's mantra, and thus the words she'd lived her life by. He'd been on her mind a lot tonight. "No exceptions."

"You're a beautiful woman, G. Delaney." Chet lumbered across the cell to the cot chained to the wall. "But no fun. That's why I didn't vote for you. Too serious, girl. Need to have a drink and lighten up some."

Grace's shoulders went up and back in instinctive defense against the criticism. It wasn't the first time she'd heard she needed to lighten up. She didn't understand it any more now than she had before. Being sheriff was serious business. Laws were meant to be upheld.

"Go to sleep, Chet. I'll release you in the morning." Well, someone would. She'd be on her way to San Francisco. With her term over and her dad gone she had nothing to stay here for—certainly not the pity job offered by her successor.

Moving to the mop bucket she'd had maintenance leave at the ready, she rolled it over and cleaned up Chet's mess. New Year's was one of two big festive events that got the residents drinking in Woodpark, California, entry to the Redwoods. The other was the annual fair and rodeo at the Fourth of July. She'd been told last year had been tame because of a heavy snowfall, but they'd still had eight citizens sharing cell space.

This year a crisp, clear night promised lots of revelry. Her successor set down the rules for the night. Depending on whether property damage was involved, D and Ds were allowed to sleep it off and be released in the morning. No need to book their guests.

Relaxing her standards made the muscles between her shoulder blades ache. She glanced at the clock. Only one more hour to endure.

She'd just tucked the rolling bucket back into the corner when patrol strolled in with a large man in blue jeans and a bloodstained white T-shirt.

The man's head hung forward, so his chestnut-brown hair covered his features. He seemed tall, as even with his head and shoulders slumped he topped Mark's five-ten.

"What do we have here?" she asked.

"D and D. I found him walking on the road into town. He reeks of beer and has no identification on him. I brought him in to sleep it off. No hits on his prints. I ran them because he refused to give up his name. I figure we'll get his story in the morning."

"And the blood?"

"It was there when I picked him up. Must have been a brawl when he lost his wallet."

"Did you have medical look at him?"

"Yeah, he has a bump on the head, a small scratch. Nothing serious."

"Why is he in cuffs?"

"Didn't like my questions. Did a little resisting."

She nodded. With the man's size she wasn't surprised Mark had taken the precaution. She pushed the door open on the first cell so the patrol officer could walk the prisoner inside. "Right this way, sir."

"I shouldn't be here." The man's shoulders went back, his head lifted and he slowly turned to pin her with hard eyes. A dark scowl turned even features into a harsh mask. "I haven't done any-thing wrong."

"We frown on public intoxication in Wood-park." Now that she saw his face he looked vaguely familiar. She'd probably met him around town somewhere.

"I didn't have a drink." His expression shifted from displeasure to confusion and he repeated, "I didn't have a drink."

"What's your name, sir?"

Instead of answering he went to the cot and sat, letting his head fall forward once again.

"What's his blood alcohol level?" Grace asked Mark, leading the way into the open office space.

"I didn't run it. He was staggering and smelled of beer. It's already busy out there with the holi-day and we're just letting the D and Ds sleep it off. I didn't think there was a need." He clipped his cuffs back in place. "Do you need me for any-thing else? I should get back in the field."

"No." Her shoulders tensed at the lack of pro-cedure but it wasn't her department anymore. "You go ahead."

"Hey, if I don't see you again, good luck in San Francisco. You'll do better in the city. We're too low-tech here."

"Thank you." She appreciated the good wishes—she did—but she couldn't help noticing there were few expressions of regret that she was leaving. "Before you go, where are our mystery man's effects?"

"Property locker." He canted his head. "But there's not much—a jacket, chaps, a watch and a belt. If you're hoping to find a clue to his identity, you'll be disappointed."

"Probably." She'd check it out anyway. Not much to do besides monitor patrols and babysit the inmates. The town had less than five thousand citizens. At double duty there were six men on patrol. As a petty officer in the navy she'd been responsible for directing and training three times that many.

She missed the navy—the discipline, the control. She'd given it up to assist her father when he was diagnosed with prostate cancer. No regrets. Even though she'd lost him after seven months. She'd thought she was honoring him when she accepted the town's request to fulfill his remaining term as sheriff. Losing the recent election proved she'd failed to fill his shoes.

She'd lived with her father's exacting demands

for thirty years. She didn't need to have him here to know he'd be disappointed.

Hopefully San Francisco would prove a better proposition for her. Or possibly Los Angeles or maybe San Diego. She knew she wanted someplace cosmopolitan. Thanks to the life insurance her father left her, she had half a million dollars to help her make her next life decision.

After hearing from her patrols and checking on her prisoners, she decided to look into the mystery man's property to see what she could find. She located the large plastic bag marked John Doe, the official designation for an unidentified individual, and brought it to her desk.

The strong scent of leather wafted into the room when she opened the bag. She pulled out a jacket, extra large, and chaps, extra long. Both were of fine quality, hand-stitched. In a smaller bag was a watch. Grace went through the pockets in the jacket, found nothing.

She pulled the chaps over, held them up in front of her and thought of the man in her cell, trying to picture him in this gear. Not difficult at all. Gave her a little thrill actually—a truth she'd keep between her and the mop bucket.

Something didn't measure up with John Doe.

Broad-shouldered with a lean, muscular frame, his downtrodden mien didn't fit with his physique. Or his protests of innocence, such as they were.

She ran her hands over the chaps, looking for hidden pockets, trying not to think of the leather framing JD's package. Of course she'd looked. She was trained to observe, after all. She found a matchbook from a tavern on the edge of town.

The watch was the real surprise. The heft and materials were quality all the way; the display of mechanics and the movement of gears gave the timepiece a sophisticated appearance. She looked closer—did that say Cartier? It did. And yes, she found similar watches on their website. Her eyes popped wide at the price: seventy thousand and up. Gah. Her next search was of robbery reports.

Nothing hit.

One thing was clear. JD had resources. Whether legitimate or not was another question. No hits on his prints only proved he'd never been caught. Yeah, call her a cynic. But why else wouldn't he want to give them his name? This guy wasn't adding up. He appeared familiar yet Mark hadn't known him.

The leatherwear shouted motorcycle, but where

was the vehicle, his gloves and his helmet? Why was he walking along the side of the road?

The 101 ran right through the middle of town. Maybe someone ran him off the road and then robbed him? It fit the evidence. But why not tell them of the crime? Submissiveness didn't suit him, but he could be disoriented. He had a bump on the head. People often forgot events leading up to an accident. Maybe he was hurt more than the EMT was able to determine.

Time for a conversation with JD.

Thump. Thump. Pain pounded relentlessly through his head. Keeping his eyes closed helped marginally. Plus when he opened them there were only gray walls and cell bars to look at.

Man, he'd messed up big, to be laid out in a jail cell with a throbbing head.

Thump. Thump.

Problem was he couldn't remember what he'd done. The squat cop claimed he'd been drinking, but he had it wrong. He wouldn't feel as if he'd tangled with a semi if he had any alcohol in his system. His right shoulder and leg throbbed in time with his head.

At least he had the cell to himself.

Thump. Thump.

He wasn't even sure what map pin he inhabited. If only his head would clear, he was sure it would all come back. Then he'd get out of here and be on his way. Yep, as soon as his head got with the program, he'd explain things to the squat cop and then he'd be gone.

Thump. Thump.

The cell door clanked. He squeezed an eye open, spied the lady cop. He remembered her. The attitude. The uniform. The pretty blue eyes.

"How are you feeling?" she asked in a much friendlier voice than when he arrived.

"Like I was hit by a truck."

"Is that what happened?"

Thump! Thump! Suddenly his head hurt worse. Have mercy, he didn't think it possible. Couldn't people just leave him alone?

"I thought I was here because I was intoxicated."

"You denied drinking."

He had no answer for that. He'd jump on it if he thought she'd let him go, except he wasn't ready to move.

"You were walking when the officer came across you."

"It's not against the law to walk."

"No. But it's uncommon for tourists to arrive by foot."

He didn't respond. It hadn't been a question, after all. The low, husky timbre of her voice might be soothing if not for the interrogation.

"What do you drive?"

Drive? His brows drew together. Hadn't she just said he was walking?

"You were wearing a leather jacket and chaps. Where's your motorcycle?"

Thump! Thump!

He lifted his arm to lay it across his forehead. He gnashed his teeth at the show of weakness, but he had the desperate need to hold his head on, like if he didn't brace it in place it might explode.

"Are you okay?" Her voice hovered right above him and he smelled the freshness of peaches. She'd obviously moved closer.

"Can we do this another time? My head hurts."

"I'm going to check your wound," she warned him, the warm breath of her words blowing over his forearm. "It's possible you're hurt worse than we originally thought. This may hurt."

Her body heat warmed him as she loomed

close. He shivered. With the pain racking him, he hadn't noticed how chilled he'd grown.

Thump! Thump! Sharp pain shot across his head.

"Ouch." He flinched away from her probing, all thoughts of the cold chased away.

"I'm sorry." She softly ran her fingers through his hair.

Yes. That felt good. He leaned toward the soothing touch.

"I need you to move your arm. I'm going to check your pupils." She suited action to words and he suffered the agony of a flashlight scorching his retinas.

"Irregular pupils. You have a concussion. I think we need to get you to the hospital," she declared.

"I'd be fine if you'd leave me alone." He dismissed her claim, waved off her hand. "I just need to rest here for a while."

"It's not up for discussion," she stated simply. "I'm obligated to see to your care. It's up to you whether we go in my cruiser or I call for an ambulance."

"I'm not riding in any cryptmobile."

"Then we need to get you on your feet."

"I think I'll just lay here for a while." Just for a bit, until he could breathe without pain and the room stopped spinning.

"I can't allow that. You have a concussion. You're disoriented. You need to be seen by a doctor. It's department policy."

"Well then." She wanted to disrupt him, ratchet up the pain, all to meet department policy? Right. He had fifty pounds on her. He wasn't going anywhere.

"How did you get hurt?"

Thump.

"Where's your motorcycle? Your wallet?"

Thump, thump.

"What's your name?"

Thump! Thump! Thump!

"Will you stop? Your talking hurts my head." So a few details were missing. It would come back once the pounding stopped.

"That doesn't really reassure me. Tell you what, if you stand up, look me in the eyes and tell me your first name, I'll consider leaving you alone."

"I don't want to stand up." Why wouldn't she just go away?

"Don't want to? Or can't?"

The taunt brought renewed pain as he frowned.

He put his arm back on his head. Nice as her touch was, her insistence undid any good her soothing brought. Her goal, no doubt. It would take more than pride to drag him to his feet tonight. Possibly a crane would do it.

"Look, I'm not interested, okay? You're a beautiful woman, but I'm injured here."

"I'm not hitting on you." Outrage sent her voice up an octave. "I'm concerned."

"Are you sure? I've never had a cop run their fingers through my hair before."

"So you've been detained before?" She was quick to pick up on the inference.

He just stopped himself from shaking his head. "Just saying."

"That's it. I'm calling for an ambulance."

Everything in him rejected the option of being delivered to the hospital.

"Wait." He opened his eyes. She stood over him, hands on shapely hips, a scowl pinched between her stormy blue eyes. Clenching his teeth against the need to scream like a girl, he shifted to sit, and then pushed to his feet. Holding his shoulders back, he forced himself to meet her poppy blue eyes without flinching.

"Satisfied?"

She ran those cop eyes over him, assessing him from top to bottom. She nodded once as if satisfied by what she saw. It took all his strength not to sag in relief. But he wasn't out of hot water yet.

She cocked a trim black eyebrow. "And your first name?"

He was tempted to lie, to toss her any old name. But that felt wrong. Too easy. The falsehood didn't bother him—being predictable did. She expected him to blow her off. It was what he'd been doing since she'd entered the cell.

Forget that. Now he'd made the effort to get on his feet, he saw the value in getting a doctor's opinion. And some serious meds.

He met her stare-for-stare and confessed. "I can't remember."

"I can't remember." The words seemed to echo through the cell.

Grace blinked up at him. A rare enough occurrence—at five-nine she didn't often have to tip her head back to look a man in the face—but standing at his full height of six-three JD required her to do just that to assess his truthfulness.

Amnesia?

It seemed a stretch. Still, he had a sizable bump on his head and displayed signs of a concussion. It would explain his disorientation and his unwillingness to talk about himself.

Then again it was a tad convenient. Except why bother? He'd been told he'd be free to go in the morning.

"You don't remember your name?" She needed to determine the extent of his missing information.

"No."

"Do you know what year it is?"

He answered correctly.

"How about the President of the United States?"

Another correct response. He swayed on his feet, reminding her that, regardless of the state of his mind, his pain was all too real. She decided to let the doctor sort him out.

"Let's go." She led him to her desk, where she handed him his jacket. "I already made a call for Parker to come drive you. He should be here any minute."

"Oh, joy."

"At least he's familiar to you."

"I'm not dim-witted, you know." He sprawled

in her desk chair with his jacket in his lap. "Just memory-challenged."

The corner of her mouth twitched at his show of humor. "All the more reason to stick with what you know until you've seen the doctor."

"I know you, and you smell better."

Now, why did that send a rush of heat to her cheeks? "I'd take you, but my duty is up in thirty minutes."

Probably a good thing. JD had managed to shake her up more than a little over the course of a mere hour.

"Check that." A deep voice announced. She recognized one of her other patrol officers. She stood to see him escorting a happy prisoner toward the back. "Brubaker, the new sheriff, has been monitoring the radio calls. Since I was bringing someone in, he told Parker to stay in the field. He wants you to take John Doe to see the doctor, and I'm to cover the rest of your duty here."

"Who will replace me at the hospital?"

The officer shrugged. "I'm sure Brubaker will send someone."

Right. She clenched her hands at having her control yanked away early. Brubaker had no authority to usurp her orders before midnight. But there was no use arguing.

"Okay," she said to JD. "Let's go." She'd already put her box of personal items in her SUV, so she grabbed her backpack and slipped into her hip-length leather coat.

The effort it took JD to gain his feet showed as it had in the cell, but he managed it and donned his jacket without uttering a sound. He stayed silent on their trip to her hybrid Escape.

In the vehicle he braced his head on a raised fist. "So I'm a John Doe."

"You're familiar with the term?"

"An unidentified person or body. I watch TV, the movies. I guess that means you didn't get a hit on my prints or you'd have a name for me."

"Right on both points." She stopped at a light on Main Street and three women in party hats, winter jackets and heels laughed and joked as they crossed in front of them. The light changed and she pulled forward.

"What happens if I don't get my memory back right away?" He slowly turned his head to pin her with a pain filled gaze. "How do you figure out who I am?"

CHAPTER TWO

How would they identify him? Good question. Woodpark was a small town with limited resources. They'd have to reach out to a larger city, or perhaps the feds. Grace didn't have the heart to remind him it wouldn't be up to her.

"Let's see what the doctor has to say before we worry about that."

A grunt was her answer.

A few minutes later she pulled into the hospital parking lot. Like the sheriff's office, the emergency center did a brisk business on New Year's Eve. Grace walked to the front of the line.

"Sheriff," the clerk acknowledged her and then glanced at JD. "We're very busy tonight."

"So I see. You're going to have to make room for one more. I have a prisoner with a head wound."

"Take a seat and I'll let the doctors know."

"Of course. Please let them know I'm quite concerned."

She found him a seat in the crowded waiting room. He looked about to protest at taking the last chair, but he sat instead. Whatever his background, he'd learned some manners. That he ignored them was testament to the extent of his injury.

"You sounded worried," he drawled.

"Head wounds are dangerous." She leaned against the wall next to him. "We already know of one complication."

"So it wasn't a ploy to advance our case?" He lifted his gaze to hers and arched a dark brow.

Under the bright lights she noticed his eyes were leaf green. And a hint of red played in his dark hair. She turned her attention back to the front desk. "Maybe a bit of a ploy."

"And calling me a prisoner?"

She allowed a small smile. "Oh, yeah, that was totally a ploy."

He laughed and then groaned and clutched his head.

She sobered. "It's also true. You are a prisoner until morning. No dying on my watch please. You can't imagine the paperwork involved."

"I might be touched if it didn't just pass midnight. You're officially off duty."

A glance at her watch confirmed his claim.

"Sheriff." The clerk had returned. "Dr. Honer will see you now."

Grace checked the door but no sign of her replacement magically appeared. JD walked past her and then stopped.

"Are you coming?" he asked. "I can handle this on my own if you prefer."

"You're in city custody. I'm coming."

She followed him to the back and stood in the hall while he changed into the paper hospital gown the nurse provided. It was a small room. She took heart in the fact he would look silly sitting there, decked out in the flimsy robe. Too bad he didn't use it. When she entered the room, she found he'd stripped down to gray knit boxer briefs.

OMG.

Cough. Cough. Good gracious, she nearly choked on her own tongue as drool flooded her mouth. Swallowing hard she made her way to the corner, trying hard not to stare at all the hard lines and muscular definition on full display.

"You were supposed to put on the gown."

"It tore. Don't worry about it. Turns out I'm not modest."

Of course not. Turned out she had a bit of a voyeur in her.

Confronted with the sight of all that flesh and muscle—toned, and tanned, and tantalizing—she missed at first glance that a wound marred his nice six-pack. Still pink and edged with staple marks, the slash ran about six inches long under his right rib cage.

"You've been stabbed."

He glanced down at himself. The action made him sway, so he quickly lifted his head. "Where?"

She moved closer to point. "It looks pretty ragged, which tells me it wasn't a switchblade. Maybe a serrated blade. Or a piece of glass, possibly a metal fragment. Any of that spark any memories?" If shock value had any power to activate his memory, learning he'd been stabbed should do the job.

Leaving her question unanswered, he used long fingers to explore the wound. He flinched a little, indicating the cut was still tender. Or perhaps it was just the thought of being stabbed.

"Does it hurt?" she asked, hoping to get him talking. He revealed so little she had a hard time reading him. Part of it had to do with his missing memories, but she had the sense his reticence went deeper than that, was actually a part of his personality.

"Sore, not painful." Emerald eyes met hers. "It's not from this accident?"

"No." She shook her head as she examined the wound from a safe distance. "I'd say it's a few weeks old. The doctor might be able to tell you more."

As if on cue, Dr. Honer, short and balding, opened the door. He addressed his patient first. "I'll be with you in a minute." Then he gestured to Grace. "Can I see you, Sheriff?"

She stepped into the hall and he pulled the door closed behind him.

"Sheriff Brubaker called." He informed her. "He's not authorizing any care for the prisoner. He's been released instead. An officer is going to drop off his property."

Just dandy. Brubaker, the mayor's brother-in-law—who until today had worked for his wife's insurance agency—obviously didn't care about the liability involved in releasing an injured prisoner. Or worse, didn't know.

One of Brubaker's campaign issues had been her overspending, because she'd insisted the town bring the department's technical capabilities up to the twenty-first century. It didn't surprise her that he refused to spend any funds on a D and D set to walk out the door in the morning. Much simpler and cheaper to cut the guy loose. Even if he was injured.

"Doctor, this man has a head injury, a concussion at the very least. And possible amnesia. He says he doesn't remember who he is. We haven't been able to identify him, as he was missing his wallet when he was picked up walking into town."

"Sounds like he's had a rough night. I'll examine him, of course, but if he has no means of payment and the sheriff's office refuses to pay, I'm limited in what I can do."

"Whatever you can do, Doctor, will be appreciated."

He nodded and pushed the door open. "That's why I voted for you, Grace. You may draw a hard line between black-and-white, but people matter to you. It's not all about the bottom line."

JD sat on the doctor's stool. At five-seven it was the only way Dr. Honer could see his patient. If JD laid on the exam gurney his head would be up against the wall, and if he sat up he'd be out of the doctor's reach unless he bent in half—

something his equilibrium wouldn't allow for in his present condition.

After a thorough exam, Dr. Honer announced, "The good news is there doesn't appear to be any neck or spinal injuries. As for the head wound, I'm going to need an MRI."

Concerned by the need for a scan of his brain, she stayed with JD, following him down the hall and sitting with him while he waited to take the test. He sat staring at the wall.

"Are you okay?" the pretty cop asked, her voice low, careful.

"Apparently not, if the doctor wants to do tests."

"The tests could reveal good news," she suggested.

"Doubtful. It's never good news," he declared with a depth of feeling that belied his lack of memory.

What a fool, sitting here in the hall dressed in a freaking hospital gown—the nurse had found a cloth one big enough to fit—while the whole world paraded by. He glanced at his bare wrist and bit back a curse. Everything had been stripped from him. He couldn't even mark the time, except to note it was moving at a slug's pace.

"I hate hospitals. And you know the worst part?" He sent her a sidelong glance. "I don't even know why."

"It must be difficult."

"Frustrating, debilitating, terrifying. The not knowing goes on and on no matter how hard I try to remember."

"Maybe you should stop trying, give your brain a chance to heal."

"Easier said than done. There's just pain and a whole lot of nothingness." He leaned his head back against the wall, amazed at what he'd revealed to her. Who knew? Maybe he was a Chatty Cathy, but somehow he doubted it. More likely her soothing presence lulled him on a subliminal level. "Talk to me."

"Okay." A beat of silence follow as he watched her struggle to find a topic. "About what?" Right, exactly what did you discuss with a stranger who had no memory?

"Why are you still here? According to what I've heard, not only are you off duty, you're out of a job."

"That's right." She chirped cheerfully, the first false note he'd heard from her. "My term as sheriff is up. I'm footloose and fancy-free as of midnight."

"So answer the question. Why are you still here? I really can handle this alone, you know. I'm not stupid, I'm just—"

"Memory-challenged," she finished for him. "I know. But you shouldn't have to go through this alone, JD. You are the victim of an accident and possibly—probably—a crime in our town. It's the least I can do to help you until you can stand steady on your own two feet."

"Why?" She called him JD. He supposed it was better than John Doe, which reminded him of dead bodies.

She blinked at him, black brows drawn together. "Why what?"

"Why is it the least you can do? You don't owe me anything." And with a certainty he felt to his core he knew the generosity she offered wasn't as common as she made it sound. Not in his life. It made him itchy—both grateful and suspicious at the same time.

"For me law enforcement isn't a job, it's a calling." The simplicity of the statement did nothing to detract from her sincerity. "My instincts to protect and serve don't click on and off with the punch of a time card."

"Was that your campaign slogan? If so, I can't believe you lost."

"I didn't really run a campaign. I felt my work should stand for itself."

"So you're an idealist."

"No, I'm a realist."

"Wrong. In the real world a candidate's work should speak to whether they can do the job, but in reality the voters like to be courted. They want to think you care about their opinion, their vote."

"So you're a cynic."

"No, I'm a geek."

She sat up straight, her breasts pushing against her khaki uniform shirt. "That's a clue."

"What?" He dragged his gaze to her face, flushed with excitement.

"You said you were a geek. That's pretty specific. Your brain let that slip, it has to mean something."

"Like what? I belonged to the chess club?"

"I don't know. But no one would look at you and think geek."

"And we're back to me."

"Yes, but we have a clue. Actually we have

several. The chaps and leather jacket tell me you were riding a motorcycle. The quality and the expensive watch tell me you have access to money. And now we know you're a geek. A picture is forming."

"Of a motorcycle-riding geek with a fetish for expensive watches? Maybe I don't want my memory back."

"Don't say that. So the clues don't appear to fit together. That's only because we don't have all the pieces yet. It's all part of a bigger picture."

He found himself staring at his bare wrist again. He rubbed his hand across it. "I wish I had my watch now. I hate waiting."

"I'd say we've found another clue, but I don't know anyone who likes to wait. Hang in there." She patted his knee. "The doctor said it wouldn't be long."

Oh, no, she didn't just treat him like a child to be pacified. Even half-dead he couldn't allow that to slide. There were consequences when a beautiful woman touched him, and she was about to learn what they were.

Shifting toward her, he reached for the hand that committed the offense and slowly drew it to his mouth. He turned her hand palm-up and pressed a kiss to the sensitive center, gazing into her eyes the whole time.

She looked a little shell-shocked, leading him to believe the men of this tiny burg were idiots.

Her eyes narrowed and she tugged at her hand, seeking freedom. He held on for another moment. "Thank you," he said, keeping his voice soft, intimate. Finally he released her.

Sparks flashed in her eyes and he braced to be read the riot act. "You could be married, you know."

Not exactly what he expected. And it made him stop and wonder if he had a woman in his life, and the wondering made his head hurt. He realized he was rubbing his hand over the wound below his rib cage.

"I'm not."

"You can't know that for certain."

"No," he agreed. Because she was right. No memories existed to support his claim. "Yet somehow I do."

He wished he knew where the certainty came from. Maybe then he could plumb the source for actual memories, for real recollections. But the more he fought for it, the worse his brain hurt.

Luckily a male tech strolled up. "We're ready for you. Please follow me."

"Wish me luck." He stood, hospital gown flapping around his knees, strangely reluctant to leave her.

"Good luck." She stood, too, tucked her thumbs in her back pockets. "You've got this. After all, you're a smart guy, just memory-challenged."

A smile tugged up the corner of his mouth. "Can you hang for a while longer?"

She nodded. "I'll be here."

More than a little flustered, Grace spent the next long, worry-fraught hour gathering her composure around herself. Memory failed her as to when a man last affected her so strongly. She had no reason to care, but she did.

When JD appeared, she hopped to her feet. He looked so drawn. Exhaustion and pain weighed heavily on him. Without a word she followed him back to the doctor's office and took up her position in the corner.

"Who is the President of the United States?" The doctor started in on the questions needed to determine the extent of JD's memory loss.

JD answered with a scowl, adding, "What is

it with you two and your obsession with the president?"

"General questions are used to create a baseline," Dr. Honer said. "It helps to determine if you've forgotten learned elements, a chunk of time or personal memories."

"Well, I should know the president's name. I've met him three times."

Silence fell over the room.

"How do you know that?" she demanded.

JD carefully turned his head around to her. Confusion briefly flashed through his eyes before he blinked it away. "I don't know."

"Do you remember under what circumstances you met him?"

"No."

"Because we might be able to identify you from news reports if we can pinpoint the event."

"I can't recall. But I know I've met him, just as I know I didn't have a drink last night." He turned to the doctor. "How is that possible? To know something but not have the memory to support it?"

"The brain is a marvelous and complex thing," Dr. Honer responded. "We're still learning many of its capabilities. The results of injuries are as varied and unpredictable as the number of people who sustain them. Do you remember anything about your childhood? Where you grew up? Your parents' names?"

"No." JD pinched the bridge of his nose, clearly in pain, clearly exhausted.

"What is the prognosis, doctor?" Grace asked softly.

"As you suspected, Sheriff, he has a severe concussion and a less serious laceration. Though they are in the same general area I don't believe they are connected. Is it possible you were in a motorcycle accident?"

"I can't say, Doc."

"It's probable." Grace spoke up. "He was wearing leather chaps when Porter brought him in."

Dr. Honer nodded his balding head. "The surface bump and laceration aren't significant enough to cause the level of swelling revealed by the MRI or the symptoms you've described. They certainly shouldn't have caused a memory lapse. But if you were in a motorcycle accident, it would explain the additional trauma."

"How so?" JD wanted to know.

"The helmet protected your head, which probably saved your life, but you still connected with the ground with enough impact to shake your head up inside the helmet, causing the brain to ricochet against the skull. Probably knocked you out for a few seconds. An accident would account for the bruising on your hip, as well."

"And the laceration?" Grace asked.

"It had gravel in it, which tells me it most likely happened after he removed the helmet. He may have fallen on his walk into town. Or more likely someone knocked him down."

"More likely?" Grace mused in full sheriff mode. "What makes you say that?"

"There's faint bruising on his lower jaw and on the knuckles of his right hand inconsistent with his other injuries. Since you mentioned he didn't have a wallet on him, my guess is someone ran him off the road and attempted to rob him. He probably came to in the middle of it, fought back and took a right to the jaw. In his condition that's all it would take to put him on the ground, causing the bump and the cut. Double head trauma more than accounts for the possibility of memory loss."

"Does that mean I'll get my memories back once the bump goes away?"

The doctor scratched his cheek. "I'm more concerned with the swelling of the brain. It could be fatal if it reaches the point of critical mass."

"And what are the chances of that?" JD's calmness amazed Grace.

"I'm cautiously optimistic considering the time lapse since you were picked up. You need to remain under observation and have another MRI after a bit, to see if the swelling is increasing or diminishing. It's possible once the swelling goes down that you could regain some, if not all, of your memories."

"What are my options if the swelling reaches critical mass?"

"Some people respond to medication. Worst-case scenario—a hole may need to be drilled into your skull to relieve the pressure."

She shuddered. That sounded scary.

Dr. Honer directed his next comments to her. "I highly recommend he be moved to the city. We don't have the necessary equipment to handle a delicate procedure of that nature."

Great. No way Brubaker would authorize the cost of ambulance service to the city. He'd already released the prisoner. JD was on his own. And her duty ended over an hour and half ago.

She could have left at any time, but she kind

of felt invested. She could only imagine what
JD must be going through: in pain, dealing with
strangers, unable to remember anything of his
life, not even his own name. It must be fright-
ening. Yet he handled it with stone-faced grace.

"Sheriff, if I can have another moment?"

"There's no need to leave, Doc." JD halted
them, a grim note in his voice. "If it's about me,
I have a right to hear it."

"You need another MRI and to be monitored
throughout the night, if not the next few days. I've
expended all the resources I can at this point."

"I'll drive him." The words were out before
she fully considered them, but what the heck,
she was leaving town anyway. This just moved
her agenda up by a few hours. Her sense of duty
didn't end with the removal of her title and pay-
check. And it went against every instinct to leave
an injured man to take care of himself.

Looking at JD, no one would doubt his ability
to handle himself. Though injured, he radiated a
quiet intelligence, his stoic endurance testament
to an inner core of strength. Which said a lot. Between Dr. Honer's prognosis and JD's memory
loss, his whole world was one big uncertainty.

"You can drive him. Good, that's good." Dr.

Honer sighed in relief. "Take him to the free clinic on Main. I'll send a referral over, let them know to expect you."

"I can pay." JD stated with certainty.

She and Dr. Honer stared at him, neither wanting to question how he'd pay as it was clear this was one of those things he knew without knowing how he knew. Remembering the seventy-thousand-dollar watch, she tended to believe him. However, a hospital would be much less trusting.

A knock came at the door and the receptionist stuck her head into the room. "Sheriff's department dropped off this property bag for Sheriff Delaney."

"Thanks." Grace took the large, clear plastic bag, checked to make sure it still held all its contents and handed it to JD. "You've officially been released from custody."

CHAPTER THREE

JD ACCEPTED THE sealed bag. He'd been released. He supposed that was a good thing. But where did it leave him?

"Does that mean you won't be driving me to the hospital?" No big deal. He didn't really care for all this medical mumbo jumbo anyway. Especially the whole bit about drilling into his head. He'd take his chances on the swelling going down.

Once that happened, the doc said, his memories might come back. He could feel them out there, as if they were hidden behind a dark curtain in his head and all he had to do was find the lever that worked the curtain.

He'd miss Grace, though. She was the only constant he knew in this new world.

"I said I'd take you, and I will." She assured him. Her gruff tone made him wonder if she was insulted to have her word questioned or if she regretted making the offer in the first place.

She was an odd mixture of duty and concern, with a whole lot of pretty thrown in.

Funny thing, his bruised brain only managed to stay focused on two things: pulling back that curtain and the complex G. Delaney, ex-sheriff, misguided realist, delectable morsel. When he couldn't take the blankness for another second, he shifted his attention to the left and admired the fit of G. Delaney's uniform to her trim body and soft curves.

Her question about his marital status served as no deterrent. He wasn't married. The lack of guilt only supported his irrational certainty.

"I have to stop by my house first," she went on completely unaware of his imaginings. "To pick up the rest of my things."

"Keep an eye on him." Dr. Honer directed her. "You know what to watch for with a concussion. Wake him every few hours to check for nausea, pupil variation, incoherency."

"I will."

"I heard you were moving to San Francisco." The doctor went on. "Best of luck to you. And to you, young man. I hope you get your memory back real soon."

What if I don't, he wanted to ask, but he bit the

words back. The doctor had done all he could. So JD simply said, "Thank you." He accepted the prescription for pain medicine and followed Grace's curvy butt from the room.

Grace made a last sweep through her small apartment, making sure she hadn't left anything behind. The one-bedroom apartment sat atop the garage of her father's house. She'd already packed her things, which didn't amount to much—a duffel bag and two boxes. She wouldn't be back unless it was to drive through on her way to somewhere else.

After she lost the election, she sold the house and rented back the apartment. Her lease ended tonight.

Her father had brought her here. With him gone she had no reason to stay. The citizens made that clear, casting an overwhelming vote. She got the message. She'd been too hard-core. They wanted someone who would let boys be boys on occasion. Someone connected, like Brubaker.

It baffled her why the town council even asked her to finish out her father's term if they didn't want her to carry on the regimen he'd put in place. He'd trained her, after all. Probably thought she'd have a softer touch, being a woman. But she couldn't be less than she was.

Disappointing, though. She'd thought she'd found the place she wanted to put down roots. Everyone had been so friendly, welcoming her into town when she came to help Dad. She'd mistakenly felt accepted when they asked her to finish his term. The experience made her wonder if she even wanted to continue in active law enforcement.

Finding nothing left behind, she locked up and skipped down the stairs one last time before sliding behind the wheel of her SUV. JD slept in the passenger seat. He'd dozed off on the way to her place and she hadn't bothered to wake him for this stop. He would have insisted on helping but was in no shape for it. Why put them both through that argument?

She believed rules were there for a reason and exceptions created chaos. In the case of the law, it also put people at risk. And if you gave one person an exception, everyone expected to get the same special treatment. Then why have laws?

Her father had been a stickler for discipline and order when she was growing up. Especially after her mother died when Grace was eight. Tight-ening the reins had been his way of coping. She understood that now. But to a grieving little girl, all the fun in life seemed to have died with her mother.

And that didn't change for a very long time. Still hadn't, if you talked to the townspeople. Grace Delaney didn't know how to have fun.

They were wrong. She liked to have fun as much as the next person. She just chose to do so in less gregarious ways. Hey, when you came off extended hours patrolling shore leave, a little peace and quiet was all the fun you could handle. And a good book or a fast video game was all the company you craved.

The activity of carrying her things down to the car served to revitalize her for the coming drive. Still, in order to help keep her alert, she pulled into the all-night diner and purchased a coffee to go. Though truthfully, JD's presence kept her on a low-level buzz.

He made her usually roomy SUV seem small. His broad shoulders and long limbs took up more than their share of space. The smell of man and antiseptic filled the air. And his heat warmed the car better than her heater.

Thinking of JD, she added a second cup to her order in case he woke up.

Grace carried the coffees to the SUV and headed the vehicle toward Santa Rosa. The clear night and full moon made the drive go fast.

JD stirred every once in a while but didn't wake up. She couldn't imagine what he must be going through. Bad enough to be robbed and left injured and abandoned on the outskirts of a strange town. How much more unnerving it must be to lose his memories, to lose all sense of self.

Except for that one moment of vulnerability before going in for the MRI, he took it in stride. She supposed it was all he could do to handle the pain of his physical ailments.

Not least of which was a stab wound. The doctor concurred with her time frame for the stabbing at less than a month. JD stated he had no memory of the incident. He'd sounded frustrated, an emotion she shared.

He had to be wondering about his life—the circumstances of the stabbing for one, the accident for another. He'd been alone when he met up with Porter, but he could well have a family out there wondering about him. A wife praying for his safe return.

A wife. Her shoulders twitched at the notion. Something deep inside rebelled at the thought of him with another woman. Which was totally insane. There was nothing between the two of them.

For sugar's sake, they'd spent half their time together on separate sides of the law.

Not that it was an issue. He had no wife. Or so he said in that way of his that was so definite. How could he be so sure of some things, yet have no memory to support his conclusion?

Perhaps the amnesia was a hoax. One big fib to cover a crime.

So his prints didn't hit. There were plenty of criminals that never got caught.

He could have had a falling-out with his co-horts who ditched him and took his ride. Then he could have stumbled into town and unfortunately drawn the attention of a sheriff's deputy. Who would believe a motorcycle thug with a stab wound owned a seventy-thousand-dollar Cartier watch? No one. So he ditched his wallet and claimed to have lost his memory. All he had to do was sweat it out in the drunk tank for a few hours and he was home free.

Except for the do-good ex-sheriff who insisted on taking him to the hospital.

That version made more sense than the motorcycle-riding geek with an expensive taste in watches and a penchant for knowing things he couldn't back up with facts.

And yet she believed him.

The concussion was real. The pain was real. The frustration was real. The occasional flash of fear he tried to hide was very real. She'd been in law enforcement too long not to recognize those elements when she saw them. And there were medical tests to back it all up.

Not to mention the fact if he was a thug, she'd probably be lying on the side of the road back near Woodpark.

Well, he would have tried, anyway. She didn't go down so easy.

The lights of Santa Rosa came into view. She stole a sip of JD's coffee, wrinkling her nose at the lack of sugar. Surprisingly it still held a good heat. And the punch of caffeine she longed for.

No question about it, he was a puzzle, but a legit one.

Still, she'd be smart to take the things he was so sure of with a grain of salt. There was no sense, none at all, in fostering an attraction when neither of them was sure of their future. When neither of them was sure of themselves.

Because, yeah, losing the campaign had really shaken her. Not that she'd ever admit it out loud. She thought she'd been doing a good job, that the community liked her. But the votes hadn't been there. It had left her reeling. And feeling a little lost. She put her heart and soul into protecting and serving the citizens of Woodpark, and they chose a stuffed shirt who was more hot air than action.

Their loss, right? Except the experience threw her off stride, made her question her decisions and her vocation. Which was so not her. She always knew exactly what she wanted, and she went after it with a zealousness that earned her what she sought.

Not this time.

So, yeah, she had more empathy for JD than she might have had otherwise.

In a moment of connection and sympathy, she reached across the middle console and gripped his hand where it lay on his muscular thigh. His fingers immediately wrapped around hers, and her gaze shot to his face.

There was no change in his expression or posture, leaving her to wonder how long he'd been awake.

She pulled her hand free.

"We're about twenty minutes from Santa Rosa," she told him. "I bought you a coffee. It has a little heat left if you want it. There is cream and sweeteners."

He straightened in his seat and scrubbed his hands over his face.

"How are you feeling?"

"Like I was in a cage fight with a motorcycle and lost."

"You need to choose your sparring partners more carefully."

He barked a laugh. "Yes, I do." He picked up the to-go cup and took a sip. "Black is fine." He stared over at her. "How are you doing?"

Wow. Tears burned at the back of her eyes. She couldn't remember the last time someone asked how she was doing. She blinked, clearing her vision, shoving aside the maudlin reaction to a simple question.

"Fine. The coffee has kept my body alert."

"Ah. And what's your mind been busy with?"

"Nothing. Everything."

"Well that narrows it down. Was wondering if I'm lying mixed in there somewhere?"

"Yes. I discounted it."

Silence met her response. And then in a hoarse voice, he asked, "Why?"

"The evidence supports your claim." She told him truthfully, and more hesitatingly, "And I trust my gut."

"I'm glad." He turned to stare out his window. "Because I'm trusting it, too."

She eyed his profile before focusing on the road again. "Then for both our sakes I hope it holds true."

"Do you have a job lined up in San Francisco?" Now she felt the weight of his gaze on her. "Is that why you're headed there?"

"I prefer the city." Amenity was easier in the city.

"Me, too."

"Another clue?"

"Yeah, let's call it that." He sipped his coffee, then dropped the empty cup into the holder. "Losing the election causing you to question your career choice?"

"My ego took a hit." She lifted one shoulder, let it drop. "I'll shake it off."

She hoped.

"Good. You're better than the lot of them."

"Really." His endorsement tickled her, bringing out a rusty smile. "And you base your accolades on what exactly?"

"On my observations. Everyone we talked to liked and respected you. It was a busy night, a holiday they were working, yet they thought enough of you to remember it was your last day and to wish you well in future endeavors. You would have won the election if you put a little effort into it. They'll be missing you soon enough."

Hmm. What he said made sense. And she liked it better than her version where they were all thinking good riddance. People did like to know their opinion mattered. Maybe she should have campaigned a little.

Too late now.

"Yes, well, on to the next adventure."

"And what will that be? Do you have a job offer?"

"I have options." Her future loomed ominously ahead of her like the fog creeping up on the west side as she took the off-ramp in Santa Rosa. "A town in the next county over offered me an undersheriff position." The city was bigger than Woodpark, but not by much. "And there are always patrol positions in San Francisco."

"You don't sound too excited by those options."

"The undersheriff is a higher rank, but San Francisco holds more appeal. It's a dilemma."

The truth? Neither of them appealed to her.

"The undersheriff position holds some appeal, except for the location. I've seen too much of the world to be happy in a small town."

"Then why run for sheriff?"

Because she thought she'd found acceptance.

She explained how she got the job. "The people were decent for the most part and seemed to like me. For a while I felt like I belonged. But the election results don't lie. I wasn't one of them. The mayor's brother-in-law was one of them."

It was an old lesson, well learned. And yet she'd fallen for it again. The need to belong. As a child she'd suffered with every base change until she learned to Bubble Wrap her emotions. And as an adult she'd stayed in more than one relationship longer than she should have.

Her last boyfriend let her catch him cheating so she'd finally get the hint. Not one of her more stellar moments. Rather than fall into the pattern again, she'd stayed single for the past two years.

"A position in San Francisco holds a lot of appeal locationwise. It's a beautiful place with so much history and culture. The problem is it's an expensive city to live in and a beat cop doesn't make much."

"It would be a step backward for you."

There was that. "I don't mind working my way up, but I really wanted something more, something to challenge my mind."

And she wanted a home. Someplace permanent. She appreciated what she'd seen of the world, and had more countries she longed to visit. But more than anything she wanted a place to come back to, a place to call home.

"I'll figure it out." She pulled into the clinic parking lot. "We're here."

While JD had another MRI she found the cafeteria and got a cold soda. The idea of caffeine didn't bother her. When her head finally found a pillow, nothing would keep her awake.

Figuring she had a few minutes, she took a seat at a table, leaned her head against the wall and fell asleep.

It seemed only an instant later she opened her eyes. She yawned and blinked her watch into focus. An hour had elapsed.

Wondering when this night would end, she did a few stretches—oh, yeah, that felt good—gathered her soda and headed back to emergency. Clear down the hall she heard a ruckus going on and hurried toward the sound.

"You can't keep me here against my will," JD declared. He sat on the side of the gurney facing the doctor, a plump woman in a white lab coat with lovely mocha-colored skin and beaded black braids clipped atop her head.

He was refusing to be admitted at the doctor's request. Stubborn man.

"It's just for observation." The doctor spoke with resigned patience.

"You said there was no additional swelling," JD pointed out.

"No. But you've sustained a severe concussion." The woman responded. "I highly recommend you be admitted for tonight and possibly tomorrow. Head wounds are unpredictable. It's for your own safety."

JD pushed to his feet. "I'm fine. I have the pain

medicine the last doctor gave me. I can take care of myself."

"Sir, I really advise against leaving." She shifted her bulk to block his exit. "You need bed rest. Trauma of this magnitude requires time to heal. At this stage just being on your feet walking around could result in more damage."

The mulish look on JD's face revealed what he thought of her suggestion.

"JD," Grace interjected softly, "the night is almost over. Why don't you rest for a few hours and I'll come get you in the morning?" The stars knew it was what she longed to do. He could lie down and be out in a heartbeat. She still needed to find a hotel and check in before her head found a pillow.

His shoulders went back and he gave one slow shake of his head. "I hate hospitals. I've spent too much time in them already tonight. I'll rest better somewhere else. Anywhere else."

She sighed. He meant it. The tension in those wide shoulders, the clenched jaw, the faint flicker of panic in his emerald eyes told her his dislike went deeper than memories. He really intended to leave.

"You've done enough," he told her. "Thank you for all your help. I can take it from here."

It was the wrong thing to say. He tried sliding past the doctor, but she had her moves on, keeping him pinned while signaling to a nurse.

"Sir, we really can't release you without adult supervision. This level of traumatic brain injury results in disorientation and confusion. You represent a danger to yourself and others."

JD did not back down. "I need you to get out of my way."

"Get security." The doctor instructed the nurse.

Time to defuse the situation. "Doctor, we understand your concern. Of course he won't be alone. He's been lucid all night. You've confirmed the swelling hasn't gotten any worse. He's clearly determined to go. Won't causing him mental duress be worse than allowing him to leave?"

Faced with his stubborn determination, the doctor saw the sense in Grace's calm argument. "You'll be with him?"

JD opened his mouth. She shot him a don't-you-dare glare.

"Yes."

"And you'll bring him back in the morning?" The doctor pressed.

Green eyes narrowed. Grace agreed the physician was pushing it.

"I'll see he gets the care he needs."

The woman reluctantly agreed. She noted her concerns on the release form and reiterated her instructions and the symptoms to be concerned over.

"Mismatched pupils, vomiting, excessive sleepiness." Grace rattled off the last of the list. "Doctor, you've been very helpful. I think I should get him somewhere to lie down. Good night."

Taking JD's arm she led him away, not releasing him until they were out the door. "Don't look back." She warned him. "She might change her mind."

"They couldn't keep me against my will." He bit out.

"She's not wrong. With the concussion you're not thinking clearly."

"You told her I've been lucid all night."

"And you have. That doesn't mean you're making good decisions. You should have been admitted. At least for the rest of tonight."

Halfway across the driveway to the parking lot, Grace realized JD wasn't keeping pace with her.

She swung around to find him hovering near the exit. She started toward him.

"Do you want me to pick you up?" Dang, she should have thought of that. She'd just been extolling his injuries but she kept forgetting how extensive they really were.

"No." He closed the gap between them. Surprised her when he bent to kiss her cheek. "Thanks for all you've done. I wouldn't have made it through the night without you." He shoved his hands into his jeans pockets. "But I can't take advantage of you any longer. It's time to say goodbye."

CHAPTER FOUR

"GOODBYE?" GRACE REPEATED. Then, more force-fully, "Goodbye?"

"Thank you for everything." He turned to walk away.

"Oh, no, you don't." She jumped into his path, pointed her finger toward her Escape. "You don't like hearing the truth so you're just going to walk away? Forget that noise. Get in the vehicle. Now."

He scowled. "You're no longer the sheriff and I'm not your prisoner. I appreciate your help. But I'll be fine. The test tech gave me the address for a local shelter. I can take it from here."

"No." She blocked his attempt to walk by her. "You can't. I just vouched for you in there, mean-ing I'm responsible for your butt. Like it or not, you are in my care. We'll be sticking together like sauce on spaghetti until I'm sure you've re-gained your faculties."

Which included the rest of the night at the very least. More likely twenty-four to forty-eight hours. At three-thirty in the morning exhaustion prevented her from thinking beyond that. The night nurse had recommended a nearby hotel. She planned to check in and immediately check out.

This delay was not making her a happy camper.

"I don't like it." He declared. He picked her up, set her aside and headed toward the street. "Good luck with the job search."

In a heartbeat she stood in his way, hand to his chest. "You don't want to mess with me, JD. Get in the car."

He struck out in a defensive move. She countered and they engaged in a brief tussle. He knew karate. And he was good. She was better. And she wasn't injured. In a few moves she had him on one knee. She released him.

"I'm sorry." He ran a hand over his neck. "I didn't mean to fight you. It was instinct."

"I get that. But stop battling me." Weariness dragged at her. "Neither of us has the energy for it. Listen, I can't let you wander off alone. If something happened to you or to someone because of you, I'd feel responsible. There's a hotel a few blocks away. Let's just go there for the rest of the night and see how you're doing tomorrow."

He walked by her toward the parking lot. "Let's go, then. I'm beginning to see why the citizens of Woodpark voted against you."

Grace flinched. Okay, that hurt more than it should have. She'd stood by his side all night and the first time she challenged him he struck out at her. She understood he was upset with the circumstances more than with her. Still, it felt personal.

Following after him, she clicked the locks open. They traveled the few blocks to the hotel in silence. Unfortunately, the hotel the nurse recommended looked small and shabby. Thankfully it had a sold-out sign in the window, taking the choice of staying there out of Grace's hands.

She was tired enough not to care where she laid her head tonight. Still, she preferred not to suffer regrets in the morning. A quick scan on her phone for local hotels brought up several national chains. She went with Pinnacle Express because they were known for their good service. She plugged the address into the GPS while JD called and made a reservation.

Given the need to monitor his health and his attempt to walk away, she told him to make it one room with two beds. He lifted one brow but didn't question her.

When they reached the room, JD disappeared into the bathroom. She heard the shower turn on as she tossed her duffel bag on the nearest bed. Energy gone, she dropped into the only armchair to wait her turn. She had barely closed her eyes when she heard the door opening. Dragging heavy lids open, she watched him stroll across the room in gray knit boxer briefs.

He moved like poetry in motion. Graceful, muscles flowing with every step. So beautiful that for a moment she wondered if she was dreaming. The ugliness of his scar stripped the dream quality away. She sat up.

More alert, she noticed he moved carefully on his way to the bed. He didn't acknowledge her, simply sprawled out on his stomach and went to sleep. He didn't even cover up but lay with his tight, knit-clad butt facing her and went to sleep. Already soft snores filled the silence.

Shaking her head she set her phone alarm to wake him in a few hours to check him out. Yeah, that was going to be a joyous chore.

Let him sulk.

She wouldn't compromise her principles because he thought he was fine when medical science and personal experience told her his judgment was off right now. Better he be pouting than be dead.

She was reaching for the energy to get up and shower when she fell asleep.

An insistent beeping woke Grace. She opened her eyes to a strange room dimly lit by light from a bathroom. She stretched her neck, working out kinks.

It took a moment to remember where she was—a less than comfortable armchair in a hotel in Santa Rosa—and who she was with—a man she'd known less than six hours. A record for her. She was strictly a third-date-or-longer gal.

She shut off the annoying sound of the alarm and ran her fingers through her hair, taming spiked ends she could feel poking out at odd angles. After one last roll of her neck, she pushed to her feet. Half-asleep, she stumbled to his bedside.

Time to check JD's vitals, to torture him with more questions about his friend the president and what year it was. He was so out of it he hadn't heard the alarm going off.

"JD," she called his name. No movement. She called again, louder. Nothing.

She reached out to shake him then pulled her hand back. He still sprawled across the bed, naked except for the knit boxers that clung to his hard backside. Nowhere to touch besides smooth, bare skin. Fingers curled into her palm in instinctive self-preservation.

Already attracted, touching him seemed risky, almost a violation. But she was no longer a sheriff, just a Good Samaritan no longer bound by strict protocols. Which almost made touching him worse. Duty would drive her to see to his health.

And this was no different. Giving a mental tug at her big-girl panties, she placed her hand on his shoulder and shook. She was seeing to his health.

Uh-huh, so why did it feel as if she was stroking a lover? Snatching her hand back, she stood back and waited.

He didn't move. Dang it.

"JD." She shook him harder. He shifted, moving his head from one side to the other so he now faced her but he continued to sleep. Boy, he was out. Of course he'd had a long day.

Yeah, and hers was growing longer by the minute. Wait, why was she waking him? Oh, yeah, because of the concussion.

Half-asleep, she perched on the edge of the bed, and getting right down next to his ear, she said his name louder and gave him another shake. He shot up, rolling over and sitting up in one smooth motion. His eyes popped open, focused on her. The wanting in them sent a tingle down her spine.

They were face-to-face, eye to eye with nothing but knit boxer briefs and her suddenly inadequate clothes between them.

"Grace," he said.

Flustered and distracted at hearing him use her name for the first time, she was unprepared when he swept her into his arms and pulled her to him.

"Uh, JD." She wiggled and shifted. Trying to push away? If so, she failed. The way he held her, she only succeeded in rubbing her hip against him, causing his body to react. Not good. Her hands went to his chest, ready to push him away. The feel of his skin, the heat under her hands addled her senses.

"Oh."

"Grace," he whispered, and wrapping a hand around her head he pulled her to him as he lowered his head. He kissed her softly, slowly. A gentle caress, sexy but soothing at the same time. Then the contrary man slid his tongue into her mouth and, oh, he tasted good. She fought hard to throttle back her desire, to ease the growing passion. No easy task when all she wanted was to draw him to her for a long sensual snuggle.

He broke off the kiss, nibbled a path along her jaw and nuzzled a kiss behind her ear. She sighed and her body went limp in his arms.

"You're killing me here, JD."

He went still. And then pulled back, slowly disengaging his body from hers. He blinked once, twice. She knew immediately when confusion vanished and he became aware of where he was and what he was doing.

Her cheeks heated when he pushed away from her, not stopping until his back hit the headboard. Could he get far enough away?

"Uh, sorry." He apologized. "I don't usually grab women in my sleep." His dark brows pushed together. "At least I don't think I do."

She cleared her throat, reminded herself he was injured even though her body still reeled from the strength and warmth of his. "Don't worry about it. Concussions—"

He stopped her by blurting out the name of the president.

She frowned. "What?"

He stated the year, then took the phone she still gripped in her hand and flipped it open so the light shone between them. "Are my pupils even?"

Flinching away from the light, she narrowed her eyes to scrutinize him. "Yes."

"Good." He closed the phone and gave it back to her. "I'm all checked out." He slipped from the bed and moved to the other one. "Good night." He slid under the sheet and rolled so his back faced her.

"Good night." Ignoring a misguided pang of regret, she flopped down in the space he'd just left. The bedding smelled of him, held the heat of his body. For just an instant, she sank into a fantasy of what could never be. And moments later she followed him into slumber.

Grace woke to the smell of coffee and bacon. Groaning, she rolled over, slowly opened her eyes and stared into a leaf-green gaze.

"Good morning." JD greeted her with a tip of his mug.

She swung her feet around and sat up on the edge of the bed. The bed she thought he'd gone to sleep in the night before. Now he sat feet up leaning back against the headboard on the bed opposite her. Thankfully he'd covered the memorable gray knit boxers with his jeans. A white T-shirt and socks completed his apparel.

Exactly how had things gotten switched around? She had a vague niggling of something happening in the night, but she'd been so exhausted she couldn't pull it to mind. She could only pray it had nothing to do with the erotic dream he'd starred in.

"Morning," she mumbled.

"Actually, I got that wrong." His mouth rolled up at the corner. "It's after one."

"After one?" She was appalled. "Why didn't you wake me? Checkout was at noon. Now I'll have to pay for another night."

"Sorry. I haven't been up long myself. Just long enough to order breakfast."

Her stomach gave a loud growl at the mention of food. She covered it with her hand. "The coffee smells divine."

He gestured toward the desk. "I got one for you."

"Bless you." She headed for the desk.

"Bacon and eggs, too."

"Mmm," she hummed her approval and detoured to her overnight case for her toiletries. She longed for a shower, yet the growl in her stomach demanded she feed it first. A shower could wait, but she needed clean teeth to start her day.

"How's the head?" she asked on her way to the bathroom.

"Better than last night," he answered with a total lack of inflection.

She stopped and faced him, lifting an eyebrow. "But not by much?"

"The doctor said it would take time."

"Right." The woman had been sure to repeat it several times, making sure she included Grace so she would know the doctor held her accountable for his care. "So still no memory?"

"Not from my past, no."

Meaning what? He was making new memories? Like kissing her? There'd been kissing in her dream. She narrowed her gaze on his face. His expression gave nothing away. Dang it. How did she get in his bed anyway? Exhaustion really knocked her out last night. The last thing she remembered was admiring his tight bum in soft gray.

And then her alarm went off.

And OMG. He'd kissed her. It hadn't been a dream at all. He'd kissed her and then pushed her away.

Without looking at him, she ducked into the bathroom and closed the door. Amnesia looked pretty good right about now. She wouldn't mind losing a few minutes of memory. Actually just a few details.

She inhaled a deep breath, forcing herself to calm down. So he'd kissed her. No need to freak out. He'd come to his senses and apologized. No harm done.

Yep, that was her story and she was sticking to it.

Back in the room and sipping coffee between bites of bacon and eggs, Grace worried over what else might have happened during the night. The fact she still wore her clothes from yesterday was a big clue, and frankly a huge relief. At least nothing too compromising happened between them.

Well, if she discounted the kiss. And she did. Discount it. In fact, in her mind it never happened. A dream never to be discussed or brought to mind.

Yeah, right. Even after brushing her teeth she felt him on her lips.

"I meant to move on to San Francisco today, but since we slept in I think it'd be best to take it easy. Give you a day to recuperate. We'll go shopping, get you another set of clothes."

"Okay, this is not going to work for me." He set his paper mug aside and crossed his arms over his impressive chest.

"What's not working?" She hoped he wasn't going to be difficult again this morning. Afternoon.

"Having you call all the shots." He stood and went to the window, drawing back the drapes to let in the weak afternoon sun. "It was all right when I was near incapacitated. But I'm thinking better now. And I may not know who I am, but I can promise you I'm not the type to happily trail behind someone like a trained puppy dog."

"That's hardly been the case." Puppy dog? More like bulldog. He certainly hadn't been docile last night at the hospital. But given his attempt to leave, she should have expected another bid for independence. "I've only been trying to help."

"I know. I appreciate it. But I'm not a child that needs his hand held. I do, however, need to find out my identity. I called the local police department while I was waiting for breakfast to be delivered. Once the officer got past the idea I wasn't joking, he suggested I take my problem to San Francisco. A bigger police department or the FBI would have more sophisticated resources."

"Yes."

"And you're headed to San Francisco."

"Yes."

"So you've planned to take me with you?"

"Yes."

He nodded. "I want to hire you."

She froze with a piece of bacon halfway to her mouth. "What? Why?"

"I may have no control over my mind, but I insist on having control over my life. Putting a name to my face is only one step to getting my life back. You have resources, connections. You can help me to learn not just a name, but who I am. Where I belong. Tell me about the people in my life. I was stabbed. I need to know if it's safe for me to return to where I came from."

"You don't have to hire me to find that out. I've said I'll help you."

"No. You're used to being in charge. If you're just helping, you're going to feel you have a say in what I do. If I'm the boss, I have the say."

"JD, it's your life. You'll always have the final say."

"You think it's the concussion talking." He crossed his arms over his chest.

"I think you're trying to survive in a world that's suddenly foreign." Not so calm now. She set her fork down. "I'm not your enemy."

"I know." The intensity in his eyes didn't waiver. "We need to do this my way, Grace."

She could see they did. It was his way of making sense of what was happening to him. Of coping. She understood—probably more today than yesterday—the drive to control the areas of his life he could. And he wasn't wrong about her having an opinion. The thing was, him paying her wouldn't change that.

Of course, it would give him the sense of being in charge. Which was all that really mattered.

"I need a job for real."

"This is a real job."

"You know what I mean. The real job hunt needs to come first."

He frowned, but nodded. "Agreed."

"Well, if I agree, we'd need to set a time limit. Say two weeks, and then we reevaluate where things stand."

He hesitated but nodded again.

"Okay. How do you plan to pay me?" She gave in. No need to make things more difficult for the guy. And she knew how to present her case when necessary.

"With this." He walked to the night table between the beds, opened the drawer, and drew out his watch.

She shrank back in the chair. "I can't take your watch."

"Good, because I'm not giving it to you. But the thing is worth a small fortune. It can fund my search."

"You intend to pawn it?"

"Can you think of a better way to get fast cash? I can't continue to live off your charity."

"I can afford it." She assured him. She had a healthy savings account before leaving the navy. And now she had the life insurance money from her dad as well as the funds from the sale of his house. Once she found the right job, she planned to use the money to buy a house and put down some permanent roots.

But she had enough to help out a person in need.

"Save your money, Grace. You're unemployed. I'm not going to mooch off you."

"Well, pawning isn't the answer either. You won't get what the watch is worth. And you can't just sell it. A piece like that would require provenance. Plus, what if it has sentimental value?"

"I don't think so." He set the watch on the desk beside her plate. "Not many people can afford seventy thousand dollars' worth of sentiment. This is a flash piece, meant to intimidate and impress."

"You do know you're talking about yourself?"

"Maybe." He ran a finger over the glass front of the expensive piece. "I like the exposed gears."

"Well, you are a geek."

A small smile lifted the corner of his mouth. "So I am."

"We'll find a jeweler." She lifted the watch and examined the craftsmanship. It really was beautiful. "In San Francisco, not here. You'll get more for it in a bigger city. We'll get an estimate of the watch's value, and I'll buy it off you. When we get you home, you can buy it back if you want to, or I can sell it and get my money back."

With narrowed eyes and a clenched jaw, he looked as if he wanted to protest. Instead he nodded.

"I can live with that deal. Let's get going." He sat on the end of the bed and reached for his boots.

"No." She leaned back in her chair and took a fortifying sip of coffee to prepare for her first battle. "I know you're anxious to move forward, but I'm not ready to walk out the door. I have to shower and change. And today is a holiday. A lot of places are closed on New Year's Day. Plus we're going to have to pay for the hotel for another night anyway, so I suggest we do a little more recuperating today. Maybe shop for some clothes for you. We can put together a plan for when we get to San Francisco tomorrow."

He propped his hands at his sides. "You seem to have missed the part where I'm the boss now."

"Not when it comes to your health." She corrected. Best to be clear with him, because on this she wouldn't bend. "Let me clarify. As far as my services are involved, there's no compromising when it comes to your health. If I feel you're pushing it, I'll call a halt. I said that I'd be responsible for you and I take my duties seriously."

"So I've noticed." He tossed his boot down. "What happened to it's my life and the final decision is mine?"

"Still applies. Except when you're being bull-headed about your health. Today we rest. Tomorrow is up to you."

"You'll make some phone calls, set up some appointments in San Francisco?"

"Of course."

"Okay. We'll shop for clothes today. And put together a plan for tomorrow."

"And rest."

He scowled but nodded. "And rest."

"Good." One battle down. She pushed her plate aside and stood. "I'll shower and then we can go." Carrying her paper mug of coffee, she grabbed her duffel and disappeared into the bathroom.

JD listened to the shower come on and tried not to think of Grace with water streaming over her body. Yeah, not working. He easily envisioned being with her, raising soap bubbles by running his hands over her skin.

Nothing to feel guilty over. He knew he wasn't married or in a committed relationship. One of those odd things he was certain of. But Grace was now his employee.

Best if he kept his distance.

The situation had already created a faux intimacy between them that created a level of trust unusual in an acquaintanceship less than twenty-four hours old.

She didn't quite get the me-boss-you-employee relationship, but he'd work on her. Getting around her unrelenting sense of duty when it came to his health would be a bit of a problem. He was grateful to Grace, but she made rigid look loose when it came to her duty.

Still, as long as he kept his raging headache to himself, she should have no argument with his plans.

A good thing, because he needed to take control of his life. Being at the whim of fate felt wrong. Whoever he was, whatever he did, he hadn't been a follower. Deep in his gut he knew he'd been in charge. The Cartier watch sure seemed to indicate so.

He refused to sit around all day and brood over what he didn't know. But she was right, the holiday hampered them. And he could use a change of clothes.

Bottom line, this hotel room beat the heck out of the hospital. If he had to take another day to heal up, better here than in an antiseptic-scented hell.

He sat on the bed, leaned back against the headboard and crossed his ankles. A pain pill went down easy with a swig of coffee.

She'd made no mention of the kiss they'd shared. Was that because she didn't remember, or because she preferred not to? Of the few memories he had, it rated right up there at the top. Waking to her bending over him last night had been a temptation he couldn't resist. Her nearness, the electric connection of her caring gaze broke through his defenses and he reached for her, claiming her soft lips in a sweet kiss. And oh, man. The tension they'd both tried to ignore throughout the night simmered over. Burned him up.

She'd been right there with him, her response explosive. He'd been ready to roll her under him and relieve their tension in the most basic way possible. He remembered the smell of her hair, the taste of the tender spot behind her ear.

When she'd moaned that he was killing her, it shocked him to his senses. Her surrender had him immediately backing off. He wanted her willing, not succumbing. If she was resistant at all, he had no business taking their relationship in a sensual direction. It would create unnecessary tension between him and the one person interested in helping him.

The water went off in the shower. And now he saw her running a towel over damp curves and that short cap of dark hair. He may have left her in her lonely bed last night, but the attraction remained alive within him.

He forced his mind away from the erotic imaginings. Instead he focused on the contacts she'd mentioned. He had to believe he'd soon have a name to replace the emptiness in his head.

It was the last thought he had before he drifted off.

Grace exited the bathroom to find JD napping on the bed closest to the window. She closed the drapes and wrote him a note telling him she'd be back shortly. Grabbing her purse and phone, she went downstairs to the lobby to make a few phone calls.

The officer on duty in Woodpark stated a patrol had traveled the road JD had been walking on and there'd been no sign of his motorcycle or wallet.

"There was a report of an altercation at the Red Wolf Tavern including a man fitting JD's description. The bartender said he hadn't been drinking. He'd eaten, paid for the meal, apparently from a big wad of cash, and bumped shoulders with a guy on his way out the door. Got beer spilled on him. The other guy tried to get tough with him and the man fitting JD's description put the aggressor on his knees. The guy backed off and that was the end of it."

"Except for the part where the guy followed JD, ran him off the road and robbed him."

"That's a possible scenario."

Yeah. The probable scenario.

"That's all we've got."

And from his tone, all they were willing to do. JD had been released. Wasn't even in town. The new sheriff would see no reason to expend time or resources on finding JD's property or identity.

So no help there.

Next she called a friend from her boot camp days. Doug worked for the FBI, in the San Francisco office. She considered him their best bet for finding JD's identity because the government had face-recognition technology. The San Francisco Police Department may have it as well, but accessing it wouldn't be so easy. She didn't have any connections there, and it could take a while to get results.

She called Doug, but it turned out he and his wife were visiting her parents in Bend, Oregon, and he wouldn't be back in the office until Monday. Great. She could imagine JD's reaction to the delay. Good news, though. Doug was willing to help once he got back in town.

She sank back in the deep red chair, happy she'd gone with Pinnacle Express. She'd stayed at a few and never had complaints. So much better than the Shabby Inn. She enjoyed the muted grays, the push of red, the modern furnishings and artwork. And the large sleeping rooms, though sharing with a six-foot-plus man sure put large into perspective.

Sitting in the lobby watching families come and go, she felt safe, comfortable. Simple emotions most people in the United States took for granted, but she'd sat or patrolled in plenty of locations that didn't encourage such simple emotions.

Before her father's illness, she'd planned to finish her career in the navy. Now, she was glad to be home, looked forward to finding a place and making it her own.

But first she had to help JD find his home.

With him in mind, she stopped in the gift shop on her way back to the room and picked up a disposable razor, toothbrush, toothpaste, deodorant and a new T-shirt. It wasn't much and wouldn't last long, but it was a start. Shopping didn't strike her as an activity high on JD's list of favorite things to do. Hopefully he'd view a trip to obtain new clothes and a few personal items as forward momentum in his quest.

The selection consisted of shirts with towering redwoods, seascapes and big block letters spelling out CALIFORNIA. She decided on the redwoods, but, of course, there were none in his size.

The man was really running on a bad streak of luck—or she was. Grace hadn't decided which yet.

Given the size of JD's shoulders, his choice of shirt came down to a kelly green with seals frolicking on a beach or a bright red with California blazoned across the chest. She went for the red. The green might work well with his eyes, but he didn't strike her as a seal guy.

Which was only half the truth of why she chose the red. The truth had to do with the fact his green eyes were distracting enough without having them made more prominent by the color of his shirt. Her mind zigged right from thoughts of his gorgeous eyes to forbidden wonderings about his bone-melting kiss.

It started out so soft and grew into a searing melding of mouths, all while he cradled her to his hard body with a surety and strength that kindled a sense of passion and security. He pushed past her defenses until her body ignited, and then he eased off and apologized.

How mean was that?

She'd be a lot happier if she could relegate the incident to a dream rather than to a memory.

The last thing she remembered from the night before was her irritation at his prime body and sulky attitude. She'd been sitting in the chair, waiting for access to the bathroom, when he strolled out in nothing but his underwear and passed her as casually as if he was two and she his mother.

Not feeling motherly, uh-uh, not at all.

Which was why the kiss was so forbidden.

So yeah, the kiss would remain a memory. Because, oh, no, she was not talking to him about it.

He hadn't said anything. Hadn't given one hint they'd spent part of last night in each other's arms. Surely if it meant anything to him, he would have said something.

"Stop it," she said aloud.

"Ma'am?" a voice asked.

She turned to see she'd startled a man and his young son sharing the elevator with her.

She pulled on a smile. "Sorry. Internal argument."

The man nodded, but seemed relieved to get off on the next floor. The two of them gave her odd looks as they exited.

Grace groaned. She squeezed her eyes shut, then opened them and rehit the button for her floor. Regardless of the attraction she had for him, both subliminal and overt, she needed to shut it down. On every level—be it prisoner, victim or her boss—JD was off-limits.

And if the seventy-thousand-dollar watch was any indicator, he was out of her league, as well.

Her savings, the life insurance and what Dad left her put her in good shape financially. Enough so she didn't have to rush into a new job. She could take her time, really weigh her options and choose the right position for her. But she was nowhere near millionaire status.

How much money did you have to have to feel

comfortable dropping nearly a hundred thousand on a watch? Lots. And lots.

More than a military brat was accustomed to.

She let herself into the room and found JD still sleeping in his bed. Or was it her bed?

Oh, no. She was *not* going down that tract again. Especially not with him stretched out right across the way.

She gave serious thought to waking him so they could go shopping, getting them both out of the room altogether. But he needed to heal, and the rest did him good in that regard.

Next came the idea of taking off and doing the shopping without him. He shouldn't care. Men rarely cared about missing a shopping spree. Except he would care. He wanted control of his life, which for JD, came down to picking out his own pair of jeans, and whatever else he decided he needed.

She wasn't so desperate to dodge her thoughts that she'd deny him his first steps of independence.

Feeling righteous, she stretched out on her bed and closed her eyes. But they didn't stay closed. She wasn't sleepy, and she wasn't usually the type to nap. Which meant she lay there, staring at the long lean length of JD sprawled in the bed across from her. And he looked good, causing her to have totally inappropriate, lascivious thoughts about her boss.

Unable to take it, she flipped over. Better to stare at the wall. Except she could still smell him. There was no escaping the yummy scent of soap and man.

Sheesh, she was in so much trouble.

Giving up, she swung her feet to the floor. Grabbing shorts and a T-shirt out of her duffel, she stepped into the bathroom and quickly changed. After updating her note, she headed out the door again.

Maybe she could pound him out of her head in the gym.

CHAPTER FIVE

"YOU WERE SLEEPING. I had calls to make and I didn't want to disturb you." She paused to look at a window display of boots. "I left you a note."

He'd seen it. A few words jotted on a hotel notepad stating she'd gone to the lobby, and then that had been crossed off and the word *gym* added. Envy caused his shoulders to tense for a moment. His restlessness told him he led a more physical life, if not manual labor, then he had the use of a gym. He would have joined her when he saw the note, except he had enough smarts to know his head couldn't take the physical exertion right now.

Not that he'd admit that out loud and give Grace any leverage.

Maybe that's what had him in a foul mood. He'd hired her, yet she was still calling the shots. Maybe his ego stung. Yet the explanation didn't fit. His ego may have taken a hit, but his intelligence recognized the reasoning. And accepted

Grace had no control over the timing or the fact her friend was out of state.

It was the helplessness that grated on him. He hated it.

For a while after he woke up and read the note, he'd thought she'd abandoned him. That she wised up after his attack in the parking lot and finally left him. It didn't even matter that her duffel was still there. He'd been totally, irrationally freaked.

At least they were finally doing something. Even shopping beat sitting on his hands.

"Good. Because I would never hurt you." He felt compelled to reassure her. "It was an instinctive reaction when I struck out at you in the parking lot last night."

"I know." She met his gaze with confidence before turning those stunning blue eyes back to the boots. "Like any cop, a master-at-arms learns to read people. I wouldn't be here with you if I felt threatened in any way."

"Right." In jeans and a beige sweater all traces of Sheriff Delaney were gone. The loving cling of her sweater over the generous swell of her breasts knocked all thoughts of her uniform from his damaged mind. "As long as we're both clear on that point."

"We are." She pulled wistful eyes away from the tall, black leather boots in the window and moved on. She tossed him a teasing glance over her shoulder. "Are you afraid of me?"

Yes. The answer came without thought, without foundation. Why would he be afraid of her?

"I don't know. When you get your tough on, you're scary."

The corner of her mouth curled up in a pleased smirk. He had to smile. She enjoyed being a tough cookie.

"Of course, the rest of the time you're a marshmallow."

"I am not." Totally outraged she swung into his path. "Take that back."

"Marshmallow."

"Take it back, or I'll leave you here to do your shopping alone."

"Would never happen. You're too nice. You need to help. You can't help yourself."

"Don't test me, JD. I've been trained by the best to do what needs to be done."

He held up his hands in surrender. "You win. You're one scary dude." He got the words out, but not with a straight face. His lips twitched a couple of times.

"Hmm." She surveyed him with narrowed eyes. "Believe it." She nodded her head to the left. "This shop should have what we need."

He followed her inside the menswear shop. The masculine feel and smell of the place immediately put him at ease. Much better than the hotel gift shop. He stepped in there for a few minutes and was grateful he wasn't wearing frolicking seals.

Grace wandered around, pulled a few things off the rack, but made no attempt to sway him. He saw a few things he liked, and then he saw the price tags.

No. He was not going to allow Grace to absorb any more costs for him. Frustration spiked the pounding in his head to a blinding level. Grabbing her hand, he pulled her from the store.

"Where are we going?" she demanded. "Didn't you see anything you liked?"

"We're finding a jewelry store. I want my own money." He stopped at a directory, scanned the specialty listing and turned back the way they came.

Resistance yanked at his hand as Grace dragged

her feet. "We agreed you'd get a better estimate for the watch in San Francisco."

"I need money now." He didn't stop. And he didn't let go.

"You can pay me back." She caught up to him, worked at freeing her hand. He held on.

"No."

"JD."

"No."

"Can we at least talk about this?" She swerved toward the food court coming up on their right. "Let's get some lunch and discuss it."

He hauled her back to his side. "No. We can eat after."

"Okay." A touch of temper vibrated through the word. "You're going to want to stop yanking me around like a yo-yo."

"You'd be fine if you stopped fighting me." He spotted the jewelry store up ahead and quickened his step. "I'm the boss, remember?"

"Yeah, well. I don't usually hold hands with my employers."

"We're a small operation." He ran his thumb over the soft skin of her wrist just to mess with her. "I like to keep things intimate."

He felt the frost in her glare sting his skin

but ignored it as they reached their destination. "We're here."

"Good afternoon and Happy New Year's." A tall, thin woman with black hair, a black dress and black pumps greeted them as soon as they stepped inside. "I bet I can guess what you're looking for." She clapped her hands. "And don't you make a lovely couple? Goodness, what beautiful babies the two of you will make together. Engagement rings are right over here."

She headed toward a glass case loaded with glittering diamonds.

JD followed.

Grace continued to yank at her hand.

"There must have been some enchantment in the air this New Year's." The woman rounded the case. "You're the third couple to come in today."

"Oh, no." Grace stated emphatically. She gave a mighty tug to free herself. He let go, and then had to catch her elbow to keep her from falling. Stepping away, she stood at attention. "We're not engaged."

"Oh." The woman—her name badge read Monique—looked back and forth between him and Grace. Finally she nodded and gave them a knowing smile. "Maybe for Valentine's Day?"

Grace's cheeks turned red. "No, not for Valentine's Day."

Monique smirked and held up her hands in surrender. "What can I do for you today?"

"I'd like to get this watch appraised." He unlatched the watch and set it on the glass counter. "It's a Cartier."

"Goodness, a Cartier." Monique picked up the timepiece and studied it. "I've never seen one outside of catalogs. Oh, my, it's gorgeous. Val will love this. He'll be the one to appraise it for you. He's out to lunch but should be back shortly. Do you have proof of purchase?"

"Not on me." He didn't hesitate, didn't look at Grace. "Do I need it to get an appraisal?"

"Not for an appraisal, no. If you wanted to sell it, you would. The owner requires it on high-price items like this."

"Your discretion is admirable."

Monique smiled as if he'd flattered her personally. "Thank you." She held up the watch. "Should I hold on to this for Val to look at?"

"No." JD took it from her. "We'll come back. Thank you for your help."

Placing a hand in the small of Grace's back, he ushered her from the store.

"Wait." This time it was her grabbing his hand. "I know you're frustrated, but it's for the best. I have a contact I trust looking into the resale value. I should hear from him soon. A jeweler could say anything and you wouldn't know any better."

She was right. And it annoyed him that he hadn't thought of the need for information before negotiation. It only made sense. It was a standard business practice and something he should have known.

Maybe the concussion did mess with his head.

"Okay." He agreed.

She nodded her approval and made for the food court.

He didn't budge and she jerked to a stop when she couldn't go any farther.

"What now?

"Not the food court. We're not spending any more money until I can buy."

"That's ridiculous. It's just lunch. And I'm hungry."

"Make it quick, then." He walked to a slated bench and sat. "Because we're doing this my way."

"You're being unreasonable." She sat next to

him and drew out her phone and sent a text. "And stubborn. I think we've definitely found your first character trait."

"You say that like it's a bad thing." He let his head drop back and closed his eyes. Immediately the soft scent of her filled his senses. Orange blossoms and a hint of ginger, sweetness with a hint of depth. It suited her. And enticed him. Each breath helped to soothe the pain beating at his skull.

She laughed, not a pleasant sound. "Says the stubborn one."

"Sweet thing, you aren't in a position to toss stones." He opened his eyes to see her glance up from her phone.

"What's that mean?"

"It means you could teach stubborn lessons to a mule. Miss I-Won't-Compromise-On-My-Responsibilities."

Rolling her eyes, she went back to her watch search. "That's called having a sense of duty."

"Yeah, you keep telling yourself that." He propped his head on a closed fist.

"JD?"

A different quality in her voice and a soft hand on his arm drew him around to her. Blue eyes measured him. "Are you okay?" she demanded. "When was the last time you took your pain medicine?"

He stabbed her with a glare. "And I give you exhibit A."

"I'm serious."

"So am I."

She swiveled on her hips to face him. "I can see you're in pain."

Nice hips encased in blue denim. "I haven't been out of pain since I woke up on the side of the road."

"Which is no reason to be a martyr."

"I don't need it." Rather than look at her he turned his attention to the hat kiosk in front of him, to the rows of caps denoting NFL, NBA and other sports teams. He wondered if he had a team he supported.

"Listen, I know you're hot to find out who you are, but knowing your name won't mean a whole lot if you don't have your memories. When you push it, you may be delaying your recovery."

"I can't just sit around doing nothing." The pounding in his head escalated. He pulled his gaze away from the silver fangs on the football cap of the Las Vegas Strikers. Focused on the beige terrazzo flooring instead. "My mind doesn't shut off when I'm not moving around. It's constantly seeking information that's not there. That hurts more than staying occupied."

"Okay. I get that. But you need to rest, to heal, especially in these first few days." She leaned back on the bench and stared out at the post-holiday shoppers. "Obviously the money thing bothers you. I get that, too. You must feel helpless without funds of your own. Why don't I give you an advance until we get it appraised?"

"No." She was too generous, too trusting. How could she know he wasn't making this whole thing up to take advantage of her? As it was, he already owed her too much. Didn't like the fact she was lending him money at all. The watch meant nothing to him. He'd rather sell it and have his own resources.

"Yes." She countered. "It'll only be a few hundred dollars today, because that's my ATM limit."

Not waiting for a response from him, she got up and walked away. About a hundred feet up she stepped into an alcove. A few minutes later she was headed back to him.

The woman had no sense of self-preservation at all. Didn't she understand the risks she was taking with him? She'd been a law enforcement officer. She should know better.

When she held out the money, he folded his arms across his chest and refused to take it.

"Nothing is easy with you. I'm not giving you anything I'm not willing to lose. So far. We may have to work out incremental payments for the watch."

Okay, that made him feel slightly better. But he still didn't reach for the money. His resistance didn't deter her. She rolled the bills up, tucked them in the crook of his elbow and walked away.

"Whatever," she tossed over her shoulder. "I'm getting something to eat."

And she had the nerve to call him stubborn.

He was the one with the concussion, but she was the one not thinking right.

She had no reason to trust him. No reason to put her money at risk. Such generosity of spirit was foreign to him. Who knew who he'd be when he got his memory back? He could be a scumbag willing to prey on gullible fools.

Lord, he prayed he wasn't a scumbag. If that turned out to be the case, better he never regain his memory. Then he'd have a chance to start over. The question then was would his true character bleed through to his new identity?

It was too much to contemplate when his head felt ready to explode.

So yeah, he'd give in, but only on his terms.

He followed her into the food court. Bought a plate of Chinese food—he had to admit it felt good to have money in his pocket—and joined her at a table in the communal dining area.

"Here." He held his watch out to her.

She just looked at him.

"You've lent me money using the watch as collateral. You need to hold on to the collateral."

She finished a bite of pasta. "That's not necessary."

"Yes, it is." He stared her down.

"All right." She took the watch and buckled it on. "If it'll make you happy." At its tightest point it dangled on her wrist like a bulky bracelet. He'd have to add another notch.

"It does make me happy." He felt it in the easing of the tension in his shoulders, which emphasized the throbbing in his head. Giving in to the pain, he pulled out his prescription bottle.

Grace watched in silence as he popped a pain

pill with a sip of soda. At least she didn't gloat. Putting up with stubborn was bad enough.

"So you like Chinese?"

"Yeah. This is pretty good."

"And spicy. Risky, going with the kung pao chicken."

"I can handle it." He dug in, savoring the heat, the garlic, the nuttiness.

"How did you know you'd like it?" She wondered.

He shrugged. "One of those things I know without knowing how."

"So the real you *is* coming through. That has to be good, right?"

Another shrug. Who knew?

She cocked her head to the left. "There's a movie theater. You want to get out of your head? Let's go see a movie. Killing a couple of hours in a dark cinema should occupy you and still be restful."

"Yeah, we could do that." He stood and gathered their trash. "As long as it's not some chick flick."

"I like a good chick flick, but I was thinking something more shoot-'em-up."

"You like action-adventure?"

"I do. And sci-fi. But not horror."

In front of the theater, he surveyed the choices while she did the same.

They both chose the same one, her voice echoing his by a beat. He met her gaze, both brows lifted.

She grinned. And led the way inside, denim hips swaying.

A smile tugged at the corner of his mouth. He liked this idea better by the minute.

The mall shops were closed when they got out of the movie. So she took him to Walmart instead. The break seemed to settle him. And he was able to get everything he needed at prices that didn't make his head hurt, or so he said.

Afterward he wanted to take her to a nice steak dinner. They compromised on a decent dinner, and then she drove them back to their room, where they both fell asleep watching a *Breaking Bad* marathon.

Sunday morning he surprised her by joining her in church. She heard him saying The Lord's Prayer, so he'd been involved in religion at some point in his life.

They arrived in San Francisco midafternoon.

Grace booked them into another Pinnacle Express, this time two rooms. JD looked out over the city and said it looked familiar. She refrained from asking how.

Her friend came through with a value for the watch of sixty to ninety thousand, depending on the condition of the watch. Rather than rush out to find a jewelry store, JD suggested another movie, followed by dinner in Chinatown.

Monday morning she knocked on JD's door. He let her in. The drapes were open to a view of the bay and a slice of the Golden Gate Bridge. He wore his new jeans and a blue knit shirt that brought out the green of his eyes.

"How are you doing this morning?"

He ignored the question. "I told you the city felt familiar. I went downstairs and gathered up some brochures. Nothing stood out to me, except to confirm I know the city. For the last hour I've been scouring the *San Francisco Chronicle*, looking through back articles hoping something would click." He shook his head, indicating a lack of success. "I must wear glasses. It was hard to focus on the computer."

"It's the concussion." When he just shook his head, she moved on. "Are you ready to go?" They had a meeting with her friend Doug at the FBI. "We're a little early, but I don't know the area."

"Sounds good." He closed up the computer.

She considered taking a cab, because driving in San Francisco was insane. Parking was worse and required you have an offshore account. But she preferred to have her own vehicle.

Downstairs JD held the door for her and then walked around to slide in beside her. The roomy Escape felt cramped, with his big body taking up most of the space. His scent filled the air around them. To distract herself from the fact that only inches separated her from him, she watched as he took in the sights of the city.

"Anything look familiar?" she asked.

"All of it." He confirmed. "Just like with the brochures. I know the layout of the town. I can tell you where the theater district is. Where to get great seafood. But I don't know in what context I know it. Whether I lived here, worked here, traveled here. It's all a blank."

"Don't force it," she cautioned him. "The doctor said you should let the knowledge come to you."

"I'm trying." He leaned his head back, closed his eyes.

She glanced at the GPS and saw they were nearing their destination.

"Head for the Pinnacle Hotel," JD said. He opened his eyes and explained, "It's near Union Station, only a few blocks from Golden Gate Avenue, and there's a Sullivan's Jewels in the lobby. I want to see if they can give me a more exact appraisal."

"Okay." Grace checked the Cartier strapped to her wrist and decided they had time. At the hotel she pulled into valet parking, gathered her purse and jacket and exited, handing the attendant her keys before joining JD. He placed his hand on the small of her back and escorted her inside.

"Good afternoon, sir," the doorman greeted him. The Pinnacle Hotel was the five-star version of the Pinnacle Express. The liveried doorman held the door for them to enter.

Inside, a stunning water feature welcomed them. The lobby buzzed with activity as people came and went and stopped to conduct business or simply to chat.

JD didn't linger, escorting her directly into Sullivan's Jewels. The store had a traditional feel. Everything gleamed, from the dark woods and glass display cases, to the gold-and-crystal accessories. And inside the cases: sparkle, sparkle, sparkle.

"Good afternoon, sir." A personable young man in his twenties crossed the floor to greet them. "I'm Christopher. How can I help you today?"

"I'd like to get a watch appraised." JD held up the watch she'd given back to him on the trip across the lobby.

"Certainly, sir. May I ask, was there something wrong with the piece?"

"No. I'm thinking of selling it."

"Of course. We can handle that for you." The young man assured him. "This way, please." He directed them to a private room furnished with leather chairs and a small table. "Please wait here. Can I get you some refreshments? Water? Coffee?"

"No, thanks. If we could make this quick, I'd appreciate it." JD slid into a leather chair. "We have to leave for an appointment in thirty minutes."

"Absolutely, sir. I'll get with the manager and be back in a few minutes."

"Well, you can't fault the service." Grace sank into her own chair. "He's eager, but I don't get a bad vibe off him."

"It's a reputable store. We'll get a fair appraisal here. Too bad they won't actually buy it. He didn't mention proof of purchase, but I don't see Sullivan's cutting corners."

"Me neither." She sighed, suffering from diamond envy. "We strolled by some gorgeous pieces."

"Huh." She felt his gaze like a touch as it ran over her. "You don't strike me as being big on bling."

"I'm not usually," she agreed. "But I don't generally spend so much time in jewelry stores. All this temptation coming my way, I might become a convert."

"If it turns out I'm rich, when this is over you can pick something out and I'll get it for you as a bonus."

"I'm not hinting, JD. You're already paying me when it's not necessary. I don't need a bonus on top of a wage."

"A bonus isn't about need." Elbow propped on the table, he massaged his temples with one hand. "It's about appreciation."

"Are you okay?"

"I'm fine. I think I've been to this hotel before. My head is throbbing and I've noticed a pattern.

My head hurts more when my mind is struggling to assimilate something it recognizes but can't place."

"Wow, that could be helpful." And painful, though it made sense in a way. "If you think you've been to the hotel, maybe someone at the front desk would remember you."

"Doubtful. Do you know how many people must go through here in a year?"

"You're probably right." But it might be worth a try if time allowed. In an investigation you followed up on every lead. She'd gotten results when the odds were worse. "Why don't you close your eyes while we wait?"

"Don't baby me, Grace."

She rolled her eyes. As if that was possible.

To keep from fussing at him, she texted Doug to let him know she and JD were in the area and would be on time for their appointment. Doug texted back to come on over, he could see them at any time.

"Doug is ready for us when we finish here," she passed on to JD. She snapped a picture of his profile and then requested he look at her. Once he complied, she snapped a facial shot and forwarded both to her friend.

"What are you doing?" JD demanded.

"I sent your pictures to Doug. Maybe he can get started without us."

"Good idea." The news perked him up. "We'll give it five more minutes and then leave. We can always come back."

Christopher returned a few moments later. "My manager is dealing with a delivery. He won't be able to examine the watch in the time you have. I can make an appointment for you, or I can give you a receipt and we'll have the appraisal ready for you when you pick up the watch."

JD showed no reaction as he held out his hand for the watch. "We'll try back after our appointment. I'm not sure how long we'll be."

"Of course. We're open until six."

JD escorted Grace from the store.

"Why didn't you leave it? It would only be for a short while. And we have to come back here for the car."

"This is all I have in the world." He handed her the watch. "I prefer to keep it with me." He made for the front doors. "It would be different if we weren't about to talk to the FBI. I'm hoping they can give me a name and I can learn about who I am without appearing a sick fool in public."

For the love of Pete, save her from the male ego. He didn't want to be at a disadvantage in front of the sales force. She should have guessed this was about control. Hopefully, this meeting would provide some answers.

Sighing, she gave in. They could always come back if the FBI failed to produce his identity.

She tucked her arm through his. "You're not sick, you're memory-challenged."

He grinned at her, the smile flashing a never before seen dimple. And her heart tilted just a little.

CHAPTER SIX

"YOUR NAME IS Jackson Hawke," Doug Allen announced moments after escorting JD and Grace into an interview room. Of average height and weight, with average features and average brown hair in the expected FBI black suit, Doug waved for them to take seats.

JD let the name sink in, waited for it to trigger a flood of memories. All it brought was a sledgehammer beating in his head. An acknowledgment, of sorts, of its familiarity.

"Oh, my God." Grace breathed.

He glanced her way to find her staring at him wide-eyed.

"What?"

"Jackson Hawke. Oh, my gosh, JD. You're a billionaire." Her eyes narrowed as she ran her gaze over him. "You shaved off your goatee. And you're bigger in person. You're not missing." She turned that intense regard to Doug. "He's not a missing person, or I would have put it together."

Billionaire? Goatee? JD ran his fingers over his clean-shaven chin, still reeling from hearing his name. Nothing else seemed to compute.

"No." Doug confirmed. His alert gaze, which was anything but average, landed on JD. "There's no record of a missing-persons report. But he is part of an ongoing investigation in Las Vegas— an assault."

She sat up straighter at that news. "That must be when he was stabbed."

"That matches the report. I have some of the details here." Doug pushed a file across the table. "You doing okay, Mr. Hawke?"

JD clutched for Grace's hand under cover of the table, relaxed a little when her fingers curled around his. "I'm fine. It's a lot to take in."

"I'm sure it is. You're an important man, Mr. Hawke—"

"JD," he cut in. "Please call me JD."

"Of course, JD. I haven't broadcast this news yet, but the tech that helped with the face recognition probably has. I expect my bosses will appear soon. Let me just say now, the FBI is happy to lend any assistance we can. Are you under a medical doctor's care?"

"Better, I'm under Grace's care." He didn't feel

like an important man. Didn't particularly want to deal with the FBI top brass. But he was grateful for their help, so he'd do what he had to.

"Those are pretty good hands to be in." Doug joked. "She always had the best scores in first aid."

"You did okay." Grace shot back. The friendship between the two was an easy camaraderie.

"I was better at putting holes in than plugging them up."

"Doug is a crack shot," Grace explained. She squeezed JD's hand, a sign her chitchat was intended to give him time to assimilate all he'd learned. At least that's how he took it. "The military tried to recruit him for sniper duty."

"Yeah, not my thing." Doug tucked his hands in his pockets. "I'm not afraid to use my weapon, but being a sniper is too premeditated for my taste. Your game 'Rogue Target' is pretty intense."

"My game?"

"You were right, JD," Grace answered. "You are a geek. A supergeek. You create digital video games. 'Pinnacle' was your first, some argue your best. It launched you into the big leagues against Sony and Nintendo. 'Unleashed' is currently the number one game in the world, and number two is 'Rogue Target,' which came out last Christmas."

"You own Pinnacle Enterprises," Doug informed him. "An entertainment conglomerate. As well as Pinnacle Games, you own TV and radio stations, Pinnacle Comics, Pinnacle Hotels and the Strikers football team in Las Vegas. Your net worth is in excess of ten billion."

"That's right." Grace tapped a finger off her forehead. "Pinnacle Enterprises. That's why the hotel looked so familiar today. You own it. And the others we've been staying in."

"You have a penthouse suite at the Pinnacle here in town. As well as in Las Vegas and New York. From what I've found, you have no residences outside the hotels. Your official address is your corporate address in Las Vegas."

He had no home. For some reason that rang true.

A knock sounded at the door and it opened to admit a tall man, rounding around the middle. He had sharp brown eyes and steel-gray hair.

"Doug," he said, his voice as deep as he was tall. "I hear we have a celebrity in the house today."

"Yes, sir. This is Jackson Hawke and my friend Grace Delaney. Mr. Hawke is experiencing a memory lapse. We were able to assist him by providing his identity. JD, Grace, this is Ken Case, Special Agent in Charge."

"I'm glad we could help. We've met a time or two at charity events around town."

"I'm sorry. I don't remember you."

"Not a problem." Ken drew out a chair and sat. "I'll be truthful. They were brief introductions. You probably wouldn't recall in any case. How did you come to lose your memory?"

Grace gave a brief rundown of events, managing to get the facts across without making him sound like a felon or a fool. Quite a talent she had there.

"The doctor is hopeful I'll get my memory back within a couple of weeks." JD added in the hopes of minimizing how lame he felt. He was a billionaire, and right this minute he couldn't hold two thoughts together at the same time.

"With the new information from the Woodpark sheriff's office yesterday, my theory is that after the altercation at the Red Wolf Tavern, the man who accosted JD followed him, ran him off the road and robbed him."

Ken nodded, his eyes speculative as they assessed Grace. "It's a likely scenario. Nice to meet you, Grace. Doug has mentioned you in passing. How did the election go?"

"I lost." Blunt and to the point, Grace didn't sugarcoat her response.

"Too bad. I have to think it's their loss." Ken appeared impressed with Grace, too. "Has Doug tried to recruit you to the wonderful world of the FBI?"

"He has." A tinge of red tinted Grace's cheeks. She wasn't immune to the attention of the head man. "And I'll admit I've been tempted. But I've lived my entire life moving at the whim of the navy, first as a military brat and then as an enlisted. For once I'd like to be able to choose where I live and what I do."

"Hard to argue with that." He stood. "If you change your mind, let me know. We'll talk."

"Thank you, I will."

"In the meantime she works for me." JD stood, as well. His head hurt and he was ready to go. "Can I take this report with me?"

"Of course." Doug moved to hold the door.

"Good luck." Ken offered his hand. "I hope you get your memory back soon. I want you to know you can count on the discretion of this office." After shaking hands, he took off.

With the exit in sight, JD subtly ushered Grace in that direction. Doug walked with them. JD longed to escape, but he owed the man. "Thank you for your help. It's a huge relief to have a name to claim."

They stepped into the hall.

"You're seriously going to pass up a career in the FBI because you're tired of traveling?" Doug nudged Grace in the shoulder. "You were going to do your twenty."

"I know. It's different now I'm out. It's not even the traveling. There's still a large part of the world I want to see. But I want my own place. I want a sense of permanence."

"I know your dad left you some money. Buy a house somewhere, make it your base and come to work for the FBI. You'll have the continuity you want and a great career, as well."

She rolled her eyes at Doug's insistence. "I'll think about it. But don't get your hopes up. I really want a home."

"Sherry gives me that, wherever I am. She was hoping to get together, do some catching up."

JD tensed at the suggestion. Doug seemed like

a nice guy, but JD wasn't up to socializing at the moment. Of course, he could let Grace go on her own. Except, no, the idea of being without her cinched the tension tighter.

Impossible. Jealousy was beneath him. He knew it to the soles of his feet. Grace would call it another clue. He just accepted that he didn't envy. He got his own, bigger and better than anyone else's.

Good thing he was a billionaire.

"I would love that, but I can't this trip. Maybe in a couple of weeks. I bet she's getting big. Only two months to go, Daddy."

Doug turned a little pale.

Was it petty of JD to feel a little satisfaction?

Grace laughed. "You'll be fine." She gave him a hug. "Thanks for your help."

"I'm glad I could be of assistance." He shook JD's hand, slapped him on the arm. "Nice to have met you."

"You've met a shell." JD pointed out.

"JD!" Grace exclaimed.

But the bitter comment didn't faze the other man.

"You're in there. And who knows, this may be the better man. Either way, Grace is a pretty good judge of character. If she's willing to put up with you, you must be worth knowing."

JD glanced at Grace. She stood with her hands braced on her hips eyeing the two of them. Finally he nodded. "I believe in Grace."

"So do I." Doug jutted his chin in acknowledgment before reaching for the door handle. "Take care of our girl."

And now he did feel petty.

"That was rude." Grace left him to call the elevator. "And after he went out of his way to help you."

"It was his job to help me." JD—Jackson— slapped the file folder against his leg.

"Maybe. But without his help you'd have had to go through a lot of red tape and waited a week or more for half the information you got." The elevator arrived and she stepped inside. "He didn't have to have the information ready when we walked in the door or give you a copy."

"So he's a good guy." He punched the button for the lobby. "I get it."

"Do you?"

"I said thank you."

"And then you disrespected everything he did with a dismissive comment."

She'd been hurt and embarrassed when he cut Doug off. It felt personal.

And why wouldn't it? Doug was her friend, doing a favor for her. He'd provided JD with the information he'd been looking for only to take a hit.

JD—Jackson—said nothing.

She reached the glass doors of the building entrance and fisted her way through. JD followed, flinching from the light. He shifted to put the sun at his back.

She spied the frown lines at the corners of his eyes and the anger fizzled away. How could she forget that he was in pain? An hour ago he'd confessed it got worse when his brain tried to connect his past with the present. He must be in agony.

The way he interacted with others without giving away his condition amazed her.

He stood, shoulders back, chin up, braced to take on the world. While speaking with the FBI, he'd handled himself with such quiet confidence she doubted Doug or Special Agent Case noticed he suffered from a massive head injury. Well, until the end when he got surly.

"Come on." She strolled to the quick mart on the corner.

He kept pace. The fact he didn't bother to ask where they were going confirmed her suspicion. It was all he could do to deal with the pain.

In the small market she found a pair of sunglasses with extra dark lenses and carried them to the counter. She started to pay, but JD drew out his new wallet. She'd given him more cash this morning. The clerk removed the tags and JD wore the glasses out of the store.

"Thank you. These help."

"I'm sorry," she said.

"For what?" He started off for the Pinnacle where they'd left the SUV. "You were right. I was rude."

"You were hurting." She caught up to him, and wrapped her arm through his. He stiffened, but she didn't let go. "And, I imagine, a bit disappointed. It would be hard not to hope your memories would come back once you learned your name."

He shrugged. But she saw his jaw tighten.

"You don't have to pretend with me, JD."

He stopped and swung to face her. "What am I going to do, Grace?" His face revealed his distress. "I can't step into the shoes of a billionaire and confess I lost my memory. The whole world would pity me. And that's just the beginning of the problems. I can't run a multibillion-dollar company. Not only would I not know what I was doing, I don't even know who my employees are. Can you imagine the damage I'd do to my own company?"

"The first thing is not to panic." She tugged on his arm, got him walking again. "You don't have to rush into anything. First we'll read through the file, get a feel for who you are. Then we'll go from there. Research your people so you know them when you meet them. It's going to be fine."

A billionaire. Grace kept her gaze facing forward. She would never have guessed. Of course, the hugely expensive watch had been a clue. One she hadn't ignored. She'd done a search for millionaires under forty and went through six months of Forbes magazine.

The problem was he had a reputation for keeping a low profile and protecting his privacy. So there weren't that many photos of him out there to find, except for the odd photo snagged by the paparazzi at social events.

She'd probably looked right at a picture of him while doing her research and not recognized JD.

In all the pictures that came to mind he'd had long hair and a goatee. And his well-toned body must be one of the nation's best-kept secrets, because she'd had no idea he was such a hottie.

Though now that she thought about it, his name had been linked with beautiful actresses and models.

Lucky for her he had no memory of them. Because, seriously, how did an average girl like her compete with actresses and models? Not that she was actually competing. She was helping him, that was all. They weren't dating or anything.

Good thing. Because he was way out of her league.

He stopped again. Faced her again. "You're going to stay with me?"

"You hired me, remember? I promised you two weeks."

"What about the job with the FBI?"

"I'm not taking a job with the FBI."

"You should. You'd be good at it. Doug wants

you to. Case liked you. He'd help you. The job is there if you want it."

"I don't want it."

"Doug had a sound suggestion," he argued, "buy a place, make it your base. It would give you the sense of permanence you crave, yet you'd be free to pursue a career where you can really make a difference."

His insistence gave her pause. Maybe he was trying to give her an out. "So you're releasing me from my promise to help you?"

"No." The denial had no maybe attached to it. He took her hand and began walking again. "But the offer will be there when we're done. You should think about it."

"Maybe I will." How could she not? But it didn't feel right. She craved permanence and to her that meant having a place of her own to go home to each night.

At the hotel he walked right past the valet station. Surprised, she hurried to catch up.

"Where are you going?"

"Supposedly I have a room here. I want to check it out."

"Without any identification?"

"I'm betting they know me. You suggested it yourself earlier."

The law enforcement officer in her cringed at the notion of the hotel letting just anyone into JD's—Jackson's—suite. But then he wasn't just anyone. He was Jackson Hawke. His identity hadn't completely sunk in. She'd taken a billionaire to Walmart. Now that was cringe-worthy.

She matched her stride to his as they crossed the marble floor of the huge lobby. The furnishings were modern, the art abstract. As they drew closer to registration, she noted there was a line to check in both for regular guests and for VIPs. She glanced at JD's profile, wondering what he would do. Would the owner of the hotel stand in line?

"Good afternoon, Mr. Hawke. It's good to see you again." Ah. Saved by the bell. In this case, the bell captain. "May I assist you with luggage today?"

"No, thank you, Watkins." JD replied smoothly. "I prefer to go directly to my rooms."

"Of course. Let me get your key for you." Watkins stepped around the registration desk and quickly returned with a keycard he presented to JD. "We were not advised you'd be staying with us. Your suite is ready as always, but there are no refreshments. I'll take care of that immediately."

"Thank you, Watkins." JD shoved the key into his pocket. "Perhaps you'll join us first. You can tell my companion, Ms. Delaney, of all the hotel's features on the way to our room."

"Certainly, sir." Chest puffed out with pride, he ushered her and JD to the elevators where he inserted a keycard before pushing the button for the top floor. "As with all Pinnacle Hotels, the building is modeled after the silver sphere in 'Unleashed,' Mr. Hawke's first game. It has thirty floors representing the thirty levels of the game. Each floor is smaller than the floor below it, creating the rising pinnacle. We have a shopping mall, a salon and spa, a gym complete with sauna, a pool and some of the best restaurants in the city."

"Everything a girl could want," Grace mumbled, overwhelmed by what JD owned.

"Including diamonds," Watkins agreed. "Sullivan's Jewels has a store in the lobby."

"We noticed." She smiled thinly, her shoulders going back. Was he inferring she was with JD because he could buy her diamonds?

"Watkins," JD said softly from beside her, "You aren't insulting my guest, are you?"

The chill in his voice sent a shiver down her spine.

"No, sir." The man paled. "Never. I cherish my job. Everyone at the Pinnacle does. I would never disrespect you or your guest." He turned to her. "I apologize if I offended. I just know my wife drools over Sullivan's displays whenever she comes by."

"They do have lovely items." She conjured a smile, embarrassed she'd overreacted. "No harm done."

JD lifted one dark brow.

Watkins cleared his throat. "I bought my wife a necklace from one of Rett Sullivan's collections for our twenty-fifth wedding anniversary. She wears it every chance she gets."

"A wise choice, I'm sure," JD stated, letting the poor guy off the hook.

The elevator doors opened feeding them into a large foyer. In the middle of the room, a glass pedestal table housed a towering flower arrangement in various shades of blue. Three archways led deeper into the suite. Watkins pressed a button on a remote, and royal blue drapes opened to display a glass wall highlighting the San Francisco skyline.

"I'll see that refreshments are sent up." Watkins replaced the remote and returned to the elevator. "May I make reservations at the steak house for you both? Or perhaps you prefer sushi tonight?"

"The steak house," JD decided. "At eight."

"Very good, sir. Please call me if you need anything." The elevator doors closed and he was gone.

"I'm sorry if he upset you." JD took her hand.

"It was a foolish reaction." She pulled away, moving toward the skyline. "I guess all this glamour—" she swept an arm out to indicate the posh suite "—is throwing me a bit. I'm not used to penthouse suites."

The slick, modern feel of the furnishings downstairs were repeated here, but where the blue was an accent color downstairs, it dominated here. The chairs and sofa were large, white and built for comfort, despite the sharp lines of their design. A low glass coffee table seemed to float atop a blue rug swirled through with silver and black.

Across the way stood a dining table that looked as if it came from the captain's mess of the *U.S.S.*

Enterprise and was large enough to seat half the crew. Beyond was a chef's dream. The gourmet kitchen gleamed with copper and stainless steel.

And all of it opened onto the world.

"This is spectacular, JD. I don't know how to take it all in."

She felt his heat behind her and then he was turning her to face him. He lifted her chin on the edge of his hand until her gaze met his.

"How do you think I feel? I own all this. It blows my mind." He released her chin to run his hand through his hair. "Almost literally. My head feels like it's about to explode."

"I'm sorry. I'm making this about me and that's just wrong." How could she forget this was about him? So she experienced a little discomfort. It was nothing to what he suffered. She cupped his face, stared into his eyes, automatically checking his pupils. They were even but pain lurked there. "We should go back to our hotel, let you rest before we move in here."

Annoyance flooded the green irises. "I told you not to baby me." He retreated to the dining table with his folder from the FBI.

"Then stop making me the bad guy." She gritted her teeth at his obstinacy, swept over and grabbed the folder. "You have a head trauma. Even without the loss of memory, it's going to take days to recuperate. You've learned enough until some of the pain has subsided. With the concussion you probably can't read it anyway. And, no, you probably *don't* wear glasses. I know you don't want to keep hearing it, but a concussion isn't something you can dismiss. It can mess with your vision."

Tucking the folder under her arm, she strolled to the kitchen. She set her purse on the open counter separating the kitchen and dining room and opened the full-size refrigerator. No water, but Watkins had warned them there were no refreshments stocked. In fact, the refrigerator was off, so she turned it on and then moved to the cupboards, where she found a square glass made of fine crystal and ran water into it.

"Drink." She set the glass on the counter. "You need to stay hydrated. I find when I'm taking pain medicine it helps to drink lots of water."

He stalked up to the counter, pushed the water aside and held out his hand. "Give me the folder."

"No."

"I'm the boss."

"Except when it affects your health. Then I have veto power. Veto."

"Grace."

"JD." Shoot, shoot. She really needed to remember to use his name. Now she'd lost her edge. Pretending she hadn't, she lifted her chin and countered. "Jackson."

He pressed his lips together. "You can call me JD."

"No, we both need to get used to Jackson."

He couldn't argue with that, so he didn't. But his hand still demanded the folder. Stubborn.

"Okay." She took a page from the folder, glanced at it and set it in front of him. "Read me the last paragraph."

He picked up the paper, looked at it, moved it forward, moved it back. "It's referencing the Las Vegas property."

"Yes. Now read the address."

He scowled at the paper, then tossed it down. "Maybe I do need glasses."

"No glasses, no contacts. Not according to your California driver's license." She tucked the page back in the folder. "It's the concussion, Jackson. It's not a weakness, it's just something you have to get through. I know it chafes, but right now resting is the best thing you can do to help yourself."

His eyes narrowed and focused intently upon her. Gaze locked on her, he prowled around the end of the counter, the action so predatory she forced her feet not to retreat.

When he got within a foot and kept coming, she planted a hand on his chest. It didn't stop him. He clasped her hand, drew it down to the side and invaded her space.

"What are you doing?" She reared back.

"This." He lowered his head and took her mouth with his.

She stiffened. This was not a good idea. But he stood back, claiming her with his mouth only. He lulled her by taking it slow, keeping it easy. He tilted his head to the perfect angle. His lips were moist, soft, mobile, exerting the right amount of pressure. He lingered, seducing her slowly, until she deepened the kiss by stepping into him.

His arms came around her pulling her against him and his tongue swept over her bottom lip seeking entrance. Closing her eyes, she sank into sensation. Her surrender motivated him to heighten the caress to the next level, building heat and passion until she strained against him, wanting to be closer, needing more.

She forgot to breathe and didn't care. His touch mattered, his taste. A silly thing like air could wait.

He eased back. Chest heaving, he kissed her on the temple. Then released her.

She blinked at him. Was he stopping? Now? Uh-uh. She stepped into him again. This time he caught her hands to keep her from touching him. He shook his head, moved away.

"What the heck, JD?"

He reached for the glass of water and drained it. "You'll have to forgive me. I didn't mean for it to go so far. After days of lacking memories and feeling like an invalid, I needed to do something that made me feel good and that I'm good at."

She went still. "You used me?"

CHAPTER SEVEN

"YOU USED ME?" The stricken expression on Grace's face ricocheted through JD.

"It wasn't like that." He tried to dismiss his blunder. "Come on, let's see what the rest of this place has to offer."

He reached for her arm, but she yanked it away.

"I'm sorry, Grace." He shifted closer and she shifted away. He had to make this right. "I didn't mean to use you."

"We talked about keeping our relationship professional."

"Yes." He cleared his throat. "I know."

"So how did you mean it?" She cocked her head, blue eyes icy cold. "Is this one of my duties? Am I to make myself available for the occasional kiss whenever you feel the need to show your prowess? Because, oh, yeah, you are accomplished. I got hot, I got bothered."

"Grace, you can stop. I feel bad, okay?"

"I just need to know what my job duties entail. Am I supposed to moan, to give you audible cues?"

Anger flared. She didn't need to make such a big deal out of a little kiss. So frustration got the best of him and he lashed out, trying to grab a moment of joy at something he was good at. After the kiss in the bed that first night, he knew they were compatible.

He should have known she'd blow it out of proportion. The women he knew would just go with it. Hell, they'd make the most of the moment. But not by-the-rules Grace. She needed to talk it to death, set parameters, probably write up procedures.

He wanted to order her to forget it, but the heft of that lead balloon wouldn't fly. He had enough brains not to let his defensiveness get the better of him.

"Can't we just put this behind us?" He tried for a charming smile. "I probably have a game console here somewhere. We can play a bit, relax. All very restful stuff."

She simply stared at him. "You know, JD, I've given you a lot of leeway. Let things go because I know you're hurting and that the loss of memory and concussion can make things confusing. But

I draw the line at being used as a sensual punching bag. If that's a condition of helping you, I'm going to have to retract my offer of assistance."

"Sensual punching bag?" he repeated, offended by her attitude. "You said it was good."

"I said I got hot and bothered," she corrected, easing some of the burn only to ratchet it back up by demanding, "Is that the point?"

"No. Look." He held his hands up in surrender. "Hands-off. It won't happen again."

"I'm not sure I can trust you. Because it happened before, didn't it? In bed that first night."

He rubbed a finger over his throbbing temple. "It just happened."

"It just happened?" she repeated incredulously. "How? Tell me, JD, how does a kiss just happen?"

"Right. I can see you're not going to be happy until I spill the whole humiliating story."

Arms crossed over her chest, she lifted one dark eyebrow urging him to get to it already.

"I guess you deserve an apology for that, as well." To delay the inevitable he walked around the counter and stood facing her with his hands braced on the marble. "I woke up and you were sitting next to me in the bed. You probably meant to test my vitals, check on the current state of the presidency and so on. Anyway, I was half-asleep and you were there and it happened."

"That's your story? You woke up and it happened?"

"Yeah," he pushed back. His actions had been instinctive. "I was half-asleep and you looked sexy with your hair all mussed up. I reached for you without thinking about it."

With blue eyes narrowed, she studied him as she contemplated his story.

Really? As if he'd make up being a lecherous fool.

"And what happened next?"

Geez, he knew five-year-olds who asked fewer questions. Okay, maybe not, but he wished she'd bury the bone already. How was he supposed to defend himself properly when it hurt to think?

"Once I came to my senses, I broke it off. You checked my vitals and I moved to the other bed." He glanced away, and straightened the folder on the counter. "That was the end of it."

"That's everything?"

"I apologized."

"An apology isn't always enough. You can't be doing this, JD."

"I've said I'm sorry, and I am. I don't want you to quit. I know ours is a professional relationship. And I respect that. But I'll tell you this, having you around calms me. You ground me in a world out of control. Ever since I realized my memory was gone, it's all about getting it back, finding my identity. Everything is focused out.

"Kissing you is something I did for me. It brought me peace. It brought me joy. It took me out of myself and into you. And I am sorry if it hurts you, but it just may have saved my sanity. So do I regret it? No."

"I don't know what to say to that. Because a kiss involves two people, JD. It can't just be about you."

Oh, no, she didn't. He leaned halfway over the counter. "Don't pretend you weren't right there with me."

Flames flared in her eyes, confirmation she couldn't deny her full participation. She picked up her purse, and swung the strap over her shoulder. "I think we need a break from each other. I'm going back to the other hotel. I'll stay there tonight and bring our stuff over in the morning."

She swung around and headed toward the arch leading to the foyer.

No. This wasn't what he wanted at all.

"Grace," he called out. "You don't have to go."

"I really do."

But she stopped and came back. His spirits lifted. She wasn't leaving him, after all.

She grabbed the folder. "I'm taking this with me." Without waiting for a response she headed out again. "Enjoy your steak dinner."

A moment later the door closed with a distinct thud.

He wasn't feeling any joy now.

Wait, the women he knew? That was strange. Not that the women in his past had little in common with Grace—he was getting used to the certainty without foundation. But he'd experienced no pain with the thought.

If Grace was here, she'd probably claim it was a sign of his mind healing.

Testing, he tried focusing on his last girlfriend; he opened his mind and tried to picture her here. Pain shattered through his head. Nausea curled in his stomach. Dots danced before his eyes. He dropped onto a dining room chair and lowered his head between his knees.

Sweet merciful dog biscuits. As the ringing in his ears began to fade, he conceded. Maybe he did need to rest.

Grace let herself into the Pinnacle Express hotel room and tossed her purse on the bed. She needed this time alone. JD had her so off-kilter she didn't know how to act.

Her mind buzzed, refusing to settle on a single thought. She was flustered. And a master-at-arms never got flustered.

She hadn't signed up for this. She'd agreed to a professional relationship.

Kissing did not belong in a professional relationship.

She dropped into the armchair and looked out on the pool. It was empty, the cool weather chasing most guests away. But in the far corner a small family enjoyed the bubbling spa.

Her bubbling emotions were much less fun.

The memory of their first kiss rolled on the screen in her head. The temptation of him sprawled nearly naked on the bed, the surprise of him reaching for her, the tenderness in his touch, the sensual feel of his mouth on hers. And him pushing her away.

Except she wasn't one for self-deception. And she didn't miss the fact he was the one to pull away in both encounters. She obviously had no restraint when it came to him. And, just as obviously, he did. So she'd given in to her instincts to flee, to put time and distance between them. If she was smart, she'd keep going.

Yet she'd committed to helping him.

And she had. He now knew his name. Jackson Hawke, billionaire. The truth was he didn't need her anymore. Sure, he felt vulnerable, but he had grit and fortitude. He'd be fine. His people could give him the support he needed to find his way in the corporate world. In fact, they'd be better qualified than her by far.

But she took pride in keeping her promises. And she understood the desire to prep before putting yourself in an unknown situation.

She liked helping him. Being honest, she admitted he'd helped her, too. In the beginning the challenge of his situation gave her something to focus on at a time when she was at a loss.

The problem was he kept breaking the rules.

The kiss changed things. Her response changed everything.

She'd worked with men too long not to know they pushed the limits at every opportunity. She'd been kissed on the job before, but she'd managed to correct the misguided fool's perception of their relationship and still work effectively with him.

Not with JD. No chance of pretending he hadn't melted her insides. He'd called her on that bit of self-deception.

Best to end their connection now. The obvious chemistry between them would only complicate their working relationship. Because unlike the other instances of men crossing the line with her, she actually liked kissing JD. A lot.

She pushed to her feet and began gathering JD's things into the bag he'd bought. Cheap things he'd probably never use. Another reason to end things between them. They were from different worlds. He was high finance, glitz and glamour at its peak. She was a military brat, a law enforcement officer with an uncertain future.

And she hadn't missed the fact he had no residence beyond hotel suites. They really had nothing in common.

So why did she miss him so much?

* * *

JD missed Grace as soon as she walked through the door. She was the only constant in the short memory of this life.

Jackson Hawke, billionaire. How freaky was that?

He wandered the suite, taking in the luxurious accommodations. There were three bedrooms and five bathrooms, including a master bath as big as the sleeping rooms he and Grace had stayed in the past few nights.

It all felt so foreign.

More familiar was the computer room, which looked like a James Bond command center. And the media/game room, furnished theater-style in dark gold, deep brown and comfortable leather. Sliding into the center seat, he ran his hand over the console. Oh, yeah, he felt right at home.

Too bad he had no one to share the moment with.

Missing Grace, he continued to wander. He found a closet with a full wardrobe of clothes. Everything from jeans to a tuxedo. All in his size. Poking around, he pulled open a drawer and found a safe. He pressed the switch at the bottom and a palm plate lit up.

He stared down at it.

"Here goes nothing." He placed his palm on the plate. Tumblers clicked and the plate beneath his hand lifted.

Guess that settled the doubts percolating in the back of his head that the FBI had made a mistake. Something eased in him at the confirmation. Flipping the lid, his eyebrows popped up to his hairline. Cash, lots of it, filled half the box, which was about the size of a large laptop computer but about eight inches deep. A few pieces of masculine jewelry were tossed in the other half, including another watch—expensive, but not as nice as the Cartier. Under the jewelry were some papers, but he didn't bother looking at them.

He wouldn't be able to read them anyway.

Ah, score. No need to be able to read to recognize the passport he plucked from a plastic sleeve at the back. His brows rocketed again when he opened it to find it nearly full with stamps from foreign lands. It appeared he was well traveled.

He looked around to share it with Grace—actually walked into the next room looking for her before he recalled she'd left. So he reached into his pocket for a phone. Only he didn't have one. Damn concussion, messing with his head. It wasn't the first time he'd blipped on something so obvious. This one, like the others, he'd keep to himself.

Missing Grace, and grumpy over the fact he couldn't contact her, he returned to the closet, did a quick count of the cash—three hundred thousand dollars—snagged a bundle worth five thousand and then closed and reset the safe.

A knock came at the door. He answered to find housekeeping had arrived to stock the suite. He left them to it and headed downstairs. At the concierge desk Watkins came to attention.

"Mr. Hawke, how can I help you?"

"I have a few things I need. I'm hoping you can help me."

"Of course."

JD laid out his requests and received the same compliant response. Yeah, he could get used to this. When he finished, he gave Watkins a few bills to cover the costs and another for a tip.

Then he strolled across the lobby to Sullivan's Jewels. Maybe he could find something that would help Grace accept his apology. But he'd have to be thoughtful about it. He didn't want to upset her and end up owing her another apology.

* * *

Grace's cell phone rang startling her from a light doze as she watched TV. "Hello."

"Hi, Grace." A deep male voice came down the line.

"JD?" Her heartbeat quickened. A reaction she dismissed as surprise. She didn't think he had her number.

"Yeah. I had Watkins pick up a phone for me."

Of course he did. "Did you need something?"

"Yes. I was wondering if you had a chance to read through the file."

Her gaze went to the file open on the bed next to her. "I flipped through it. Doug gave you the highlights. I'll do a search for your key personnel tonight and we can go over the information tomorrow."

"How about tonight? Come back, join me for dinner."

She hesitated, tempted to do just that. The very fact she wanted to explained why she couldn't. "I think it's best if we take this time apart."

"So you said." He sounded disappointed. Or was that wishful thinking? "Let me know if you change your mind."

* * *

Grace stormed into Jackson's suite. She powered right through the foyer into the living area. The fact he wasn't there blasted her ire further up the scale.

"Jackson Hawke, show yourself." The sharp demand rolled through the rooms.

"You're back." He appeared in the arched doorway.

"You have some nerve." She tossed her purse on the white couch. "How dare you have me evicted from my room at the Pinnacle Express hotel?"

"Did they upset you?" A frown drew his reddish brown eyebrows together. "I expressly requested they not upset you."

"Oh, the manager was very nice." She paced in front of the window. "As he threw me out of my room. How can that be anything but upsetting? I was so embarrassed."

"They were instructed that you were being upgraded to this hotel. Why would that be embarrassing?"

"Oh, I don't know," she mocked. "Maybe because they now think we're romantically involved and that I'm available at the click of your fingers." Seeking calm she drew in a deep breath, let it out slow. "What's the deal, Jackson?"

"I wanted you here. I owe you a nice steak dinner."

"It was a gross misuse of your authority. I was coming back in the morning. There was no need to go to such drastic measures."

He drew closer until he invaded her space. He stopped short of touching her, though his fingers twitched as if he wanted to. "Why are you calling me Jackson?"

"It's your name." And her way of calling to mind the differences between them. Her chin lifted. No need for him to know that.

"I didn't want you spending your money over there when there's plenty of room here. The place has three bedrooms. We can be apart in separate rooms."

"It's not the same."

"I know. That's the other reason I did it." Giving her a sad smile, he gazed into her eyes and confessed, "I was lonely without you."

Her anger deflated like a pinpricked balloon.

"You were out of line," she declared, unwilling to let him charm her so easily.

"I won't do it again." His fingers feathered over

her hand, before he pulled back. "Not without warning you first."

She narrowed her eyes, reproaching him.

He shrugged. "It's the best I can do. And seriously, I couldn't enjoy my steak dinner without you."

"You could have changed the reservation to tomorrow."

"I considered it. But I wanted you here." He held his hand out toward the doorway. "Come, let me show you the rest of the suite."

Her eye landed on his new phone. She picked it up. "You need to be careful what you do. The hotel may let you slide on the bill, but you're still going to need money until you can get new identification and new credit cards. I leave you alone for a few minutes—"

His finger on her lips shushed her. "How about this—you don't treat me like a child, and I won't treat you like a sensual punching bag. Fair trade?"

An argument sprang to her lips. She bit them together, holding it back.

"Fair trade."

"Good." He smiled and, wrapping his fingers around hers, led her out of the room. "Now, let me show you what I've found."

She tried to work her hand free, but it was a halfhearted attempt, and he ignored her as he moved through the suite showing her bedrooms, an office that rivaled British Command, a media room with a full-size billiard table and finally a master suite to die for.

"OMG." The bathroom took her breath away. The walls were made of glass, thick bricks on the bottom to obscure visibility and preserve privacy, but the top part was clear, blue-tinted glass. The huge walk-in shower was made of quartz rocks and lush, overhead greenery. Multiple showerheads promised a luxurious drenching. When you took a shower, you'd feel as if you were at the top of a waterfall looking down on the world. "Dibs on the shower."

He laughed. "I've already used it. It's quite spectacular."

She poked her head in a sauna. "Is this what you wanted to show me?"

"No. I saved the best for last." He disappeared back into the bedroom. She slowly followed, her feet reluctant to leave the bathroom oasis.

Inside the bedroom he'd disappeared altogether. "Jackson?"

"In here." His head popped out of a closet.

She joined him, stopping on the threshold to blink and take it in. Okay, maybe owning a house was overrated. Maybe she didn't need to own the ground under her feet to consider the space she occupied as home. Because, seriously, she could live in this room.

"Wow. Just wow." Forget sleek and slick in here. Warm wood and creamy marble welcomed her inside. Suits lined one side split by a three-way mirror, while shoes filled the opposite side and down the center ran a marble-topped island with a sink at one end and drawers on all sides. Three chandeliers lit the room and a chaise lounge provided a spot to sit. "I think I'm in love."

"And I think that's the most girlish thing I've heard you say."

"I'm a girl," she defended her reaction.

"Mostly you're a cop."

"Seriously? You're going to go there after the whole kissing incident?"

His expression was total innocence. "I didn't say you weren't pretty."

She scowled, as mad at herself for the surge of pleasure as she was at him for the asinine comment. Shaking a finger at him, she advised, "You may want to stop while you're ahead."

"I'm ahead?" He grinned, flashing his dimple.

"Better watch it," she cautioned. "You didn't care for the consequences the last time you provoked me."

Jackson sobered. "You don't strike me as the type to run from your problems."

"I'm not. But I'm not a martyr either, so I do believe in stepping back to cool off. An occurrence that shouldn't be necessary in a professional relationship. At least not often."

"Okay, okay." He raised his hands in surrender. "Message received. We'll keep it professional. Now, look."

He grabbed her hand and drew her next to him where he stood over an open drawer in the island. She shook her head. The man needed a pamphlet on respecting people's boundaries.

She glanced in the drawer. Oh. "It's a safe." With a palm plate lock. She looked up at him. "Did you try to open it?"

"I did. Watch." He placed his hand on the lock. She held her breath.

It clicked open.

She grinned around a rush of air. How horrible would it be if he'd only been a Jackson Hawke look-alike? Yeah, it might have been rough explaining their presence in a billionaire's personal suite to the San Francisco Police Department.

And then he opened the safe and all thought left her head. She stared at a stack of cash easily equal to a quarter of a million dollars.

"Good gracious," she breathed clasping her hands behind her back to keep from touching. "Jackpot for you."

"And the cash isn't all that's in here." He pulled out a passport. "This will work for ID right?"

"Yes, it will."

"Good. I had Watkins contact my people in Las Vegas to let them know I lost my wallet. He reported I'd have replacement cards in the morning."

"Sounds like you're all set." She was right, he had done just fine without her. And she wasn't sure how she felt about that.

CHAPTER EIGHT

"Do not even think of dodging out on me," he whispered in her ear. "I know that's what you're thinking."

"It's something to consider," she countered, for her benefit as well as his. "You did all this on your own. And you have people now that can help you."

"Which is why I need you now more than ever." He reached for something deep in the vault. "No need to sell my watch." He glanced down at her. "It does have sentimental value now. And I'm keeping the provenance papers on my person, just in case."

"Hopefully nothing like this will happen to you again."

"Hopefully. But I have the stab wound, too. So obviously stuff happens."

"I guess. But you can't live your life based on fear."

"I don't intend to, but there's such a thing as

precaution. I'll carry the papers for a while. And I got this for you." He handed her a four-inch square jeweler's box with the name Sullivan's scrawled across the top. "For all your help."

Again her hands went behind her back. "I can't take that."

"Of course you can. I can afford it. I'm getting the sense that being rich comes naturally to me."

She sent him a droll stare. "Being rich and being a jerk are not the same thing."

"Ouch. I probably deserve that."

"No probably about it."

He ignored her. Instead he ran his hand down her arm and pulled her hand around to place the box in her palm. "I want to do this for you. You don't really understand what your help has meant to me. I'm bad at verbalizing it, and yeah, I've messed up a couple of times. I'm nobody to you, a stranger, yet without hesitation you stepped up to help me. Paying my way when you didn't have a job yourself and there were no apparent means of me being able to pay you back."

"There was the watch," she reminded him. "I didn't do anything anyone else wouldn't do." She set the box on the counter and edged away from

Jackson until she stood across from him. "And you are paying me."

"You don't even understand how special you are. Let's be clear, I'm paying you for your knowledge and your connections. There's no way to fully pay you for your compassion, your patience, your faith in me. This," he said, pushing the box toward her, "is a mere token of what you deserve. My hope is you'll know my gratitude whenever you wear it. And because it seemed right, it's Cartier."

"Jackson." She stared at him helplessly. A Cartier? It was too much. Of course it was too much. She couldn't take it. Could she?

"It'll go to waste if you don't take it. I'll put it back in the safe and it'll stay there forever."

"No." Her hand moved protectively toward the package before her mind engaged and she curled her fingers closed. But the thought of his gift languishing, forever unopened, seemed wrong. "That would be a waste. You should return it or give it to someone else."

"It isn't meant for someone else. It wouldn't have the same value. It's for you, or no one."

"Oh, give it to me already." She held her hand out palm up.

His eyes lit up. Knowing better than to say any-thing, he grandly placed the package in her grasp.

"You are never to tell me how much this cost."

"Rest assured it was below ninety thousand."

Her gaze flew to his face. "It better be well, well below."

"You said not to tell you."

"Oh, my gosh. You are evil." Opening the box, she peaked inside and forgot to breathe. "Oh, my. Oh, JD." She lifted out a thin rope of diamonds set in white gold. "It's beautiful."

"Let me." He took it from her, wrapped it around her right wrist and connected the clasp. "It looks good on you."

"It would look good on a cat." She moved her arm, admiring the flash of the diamonds in the light. It really was too much.

"No going back." Again he seemed to read her mind. "And it'll go really good with the little black dress I got you to wear to dinner."

"What? Oh, no, nothing more." She was talk-ing to his back. "I'm not taking anything else from you."

"Not even the shower?" he said over his shoul-der. "Everything is laid out in your room."

"Everything? No. No. No." She dogged his heels. "Jackson, I'm serious. No more."

"I'll be in the game room when you're ready." He stopped and gave her a wink. "Our reservation is at eight." He turned into the game room leaving the door open behind him.

Grace dug in her heels determined not to chase after him any farther. She was an intelligent, competent woman, not a witless fool. He had no power over her. She'd wear an outfit of her own choosing.

Don't look, she warned herself as she entered her room and headed straight for the bathroom. *Pay no attention to the clothes on the bed.*

She might have made it, except the room itself stopped her. Done in white, gold and silver, the decor took her breath away. Decked out all in white, the bed appeared to float. Above it, large gold discs drew your attention up. A silver geometric design in the white carpet was repeated on the ceiling trim. In front of the window a modern sofa and chair in a soft silvery-gold invited her to come sit and relax.

No way was that possible with the clothes strewn across the bed.

Of course she looked.

And her feet betrayed her by taking her closer. Oh, my. He'd gone with the classic little black dress. It lay stretched across the white down-filled duvet. And he nailed her taste to a T. The dress had a boatneck with three horizontal strips of sheer mesh between the neckline and bustline and then again at the bottom of the slightly flared skirt ending with the mesh a few inches above the knee. The dress managed to be both sexy and conservative at the same time.

A pair of peep-toe heels sat on the floor, and a tiny black patent-leather purse rested next to the dress on the bed, along with a box and a bag from Victoria's Secret. For a woman who'd spent a good part of her life in uniform, the ensemble was irresistible.

Still, her resolve may have held except she kept remembering the exotic waterfall shower in Jackson's bathroom. The devious man had connected the two, making her feel she had to wear the dress to have use of his facilities. Heights had never bothered her, and oh, how she longed for a top-of-the-world experience.

And by gosh, she meant to claim it.

If that meant wearing the dress, she'd wear the

dress and wear it well. Her legs were one of her best features.

Shouldering her duffel, she left the lovely room and headed straight for Jackson's bathroom. She closed and locked the door. Using the control panel on the outside of the shower she keyed in the number of shower panels—all—and temperature—hot—she wanted. Then she checked out the contents of the Victoria's Secret bag. Shampoo and conditioner and body wash and lotion, all in her favorite orange-blossom scent. Nodding, she stripped and stepped inside.

Water washed over her from all sides.

Heaven.

Well worth a small slice of her pride. For which he'd pay. Oh, yeah, she'd make him sweat for forcing the issue, for stealing kisses and ignoring the rules. And get dessert, as well. Sweet.

The shower grotto ran about seven feet long and five feet deep. About four feet of it was glass bricks topped by clear glass. The other three feet was a stone wall made up of smooth multisize rocks that curved around to create the side of the grotto. A stone bench followed the curve.

Water rained down on her, hot and steamy. She stood on smooth rocks while green fronds draped over the top and sides of the glass partition. The glass bricks came to her bust, safeguarding her modesty. Moving up to the glass, she looked down. The magnificent city spread out before her. In the distance the ocean reflected the clear blue sky and rippled with whitecaps. To her left the Golden Gate Bridge spanned the water to Oakland.

The intoxicating scent of the luxury soaps and shampoos only added to the experience. And made her hair and skin so soft. She never wanted to leave.

The only thing missing was a man to share it with.

Immediately a picture of Jackson sprang to mind. Even in their bare feet he'd tower over her. His broad shoulders would shield her from the brunt of the spray as he kissed her neck.

She turned so the water pulsed against her neck.

And lower. She imagined his hands smoothing away bubbles and his mouth on her body.

When her blood heated to the temperature of the water, he moved them away from the glass to the wide bench and his mouth and hands slid lower yet.

A knock at the door interrupted her fantasy. "Let me know if you need anything." Jackson called out. "The control panel inside the shower includes a phone feature. I plugged my new cell number in for you."

Her eyes popped open.

"I'm fine," she nearly snarled.

Resting on the edge of fulfillment, she glared at the door. What lousy timing. But apropos. She had no business fantasizing about him. Especially after the hands-off speech she gave him.

In retaliation for her traitorous imaginings, she flipped the hot water off first. An icy blast of water hit her heated body. She shivered and quickly keyed off the cold.

"Brr." Outside the grotto she reached for a towel from the stack on a nearby shelf. The thick terry cloth was warm to the touch and the size of a small blanket. She sighed as the warmth enveloped her.

Using a smaller towel—also warmed on the heating rack—she dried her hair and recalled Jackson's comment about being accustomed to wealth. Hmm. More likely it was too easy to give in to the seduction of luxury.

It was okay for him to immerse himself in this world. He belonged here, after all.

She, on the other hand, needed to take care she didn't succumb to the temptation of what couldn't be.

Jackson shot a tiger and swung across the ravine on a tree vine that dropped him short of the opposite side so he fell into a raging river. He caught a ride on a floating log and made it to the other side, but he had a strenuous climb ahead of him.

"I'm ready," Grace announced from the back of the room.

"Me, too. Ah, cagey croc." A crocodile morphed from a log to attack him. "Just one minute," he muttered to Grace as his avatar went after the croc.

"Take your time."

He caught sight of her as she rounded the front of the seats. That brief glance he got of her legs demanded a full-blown perusal. He sat back, ran his gaze from the pink-tipped toes peeking out of her black pumps, up smooth, shapely legs. The dress clung in all the right places, and yes, one of the sheer mesh strips perfectly framed a nice view of her cleavage. A pretty sheen highlighted her lips and eyes. And sweet merciful peaches, she'd mussed her black hair so she looked as if she'd just made love.

"Smokin'."

Amusement lit up her blue eyes. "Me? Or the game?"

"Kak." The game sounded, then announced, "Raptor, you have lost your first life."

"What?" Shifting back to the monitor he saw the croc had eaten him. "Pisser."

"Oh, did you die? Hate when that happens."

"Humph." He might be annoyed with her, except damn, smug never looked so good. "Do you play?"

"Sure. You want to go a round?"

"I'll take you on." The game allowed for a player to play individually or against one or more players. He nodded to the seat next to him, as he reached for the control pad. "Fair warning, I created the game."

"Not now, Jackson." Her hands went to her shapely hips. "We have reservations, remember? Plus, I'm hungry."

"Right. Right." He surged to his feet. "May I say how stunning you look?"

"No, you may not." She turned on her heels

and headed out. "That would only be bragging. You coming?"

Following after her, Jackson slowly shook his head. For someone who looked so soft, the woman had no give in her.

The steak-house restaurant went against the futuristic theme of the hotel, going instead with rich, dark woods, marble counters and fine crystal. They offered their clients privacy and range-fed beef. He saw Grace seated and ordered them each a nice glass of wine.

She sipped the wine, savored it on her tongue, then set the glass down.

"Shall I order for you?" He offered.

"I'm a big girl. I can order for myself." She opened the menu and began to scan the choices.

His menu remained on the table. While killing time earlier, he'd checked out the menu online. Better to struggle over the words in his suite than at the restaurant. He hadn't used the top-of-the-line unit in the office. It was password protected, and his head wasn't spitting out any clues to what it might be.

He could not wait until his memory returned.

He'd bought a new tablet at one of the stores in the attached shopping mall. He applauded his decision to make the mall part of the hotel. Travelers often had unexpected needs. He'd certainly found it handy.

He'd enjoyed shopping for Grace. Enjoyed seeing her in the things he'd bought.

The lighting was muted to heighten the sense of privacy, yet as she moved her head to read the menu, light flickered from one spiked tress to the next. She bit her lip in indecision, and he sucked in a breath. White teeth dented plump flesh. It was all he could do to stay in his seat.

More as a distraction than out of need, he opened the menu.

He wouldn't act on his desire. He respected her too much.

Needed her too much, come to that. No matter what she believed.

The waiter appeared. Grace surprised Jackson by ordering the rib eye. He would have pegged her as a salad girl. She kept surprising him. He liked that.

When they were alone again, he sought for a topic of conversation. Easy. "Tell me what you found in my file."

She sat back on her bench seat, and clasped her hands on the table in front of her.

"You were a foster child. Mother died when you were five. Your father was unknown. There was a note in the file that a friend may have knowledge of who he was, but they were unable to locate the friend so no investigation was lodged."

"So I just went into the system?"

"Yes. From what I read, you were passed around to several homes, longest stay was two years. You were quiet and smart, kept to yourself for the most part, but suffered some bullying. A few incidents of cyber retaliation—quite creative, I must say—got you expelled. So you went to three different high schools."

"How many homes overall?"

"Nine."

"Over thirteen years?" It was a lot. He waited for emotions to come—loss, anger, resentment— but he felt nothing. Only the pounding in his head.

"Obviously you had a tough childhood. I can relate, to a degree. Being a military brat, I know how it feels to be uprooted and moved to a new home every few years. How hard it is to start over again and again. You learn to protect yourself."

"I don't remember any of it," he confessed.

She laid her hand over his. "That may be a

good thing. With this background, if you lost your memory but remembered your childhood, you would have found it difficult to accept help, however honestly offered."

The food arrived, saving him from the need to reply. He'd also gone with the rib-eye steak and paired it with shrimp. His mouth watered at the aroma coming off the plate. He cut into the steak and found a warm, pink center. The meat melted in his mouth. Across the way he watched Grace savor her first bite and bit back a groan at the ecstatic expression on her face.

She caught him staring and a rush of red rose in her cheeks. She gave a sheepish smile. "It's good."

While they ate, she shared more of what she read in the file. He'd done a stint in juvenile detention for hacking into a school to change grades. Not just his own, apparently, but every student who took English with Mrs. Manning, who he stated was a frigid old crow who got her jollies putting down students to make herself feel superior.

"It sounds like I was doing the world a service. The report seems quite detailed."

"The FBI is thorough."

"So it appears. Can we move past my school years? At least skip to college."

"What makes you think you went to college?"

The question drew his attention away from the peekaboo view of her cleavage. "I didn't go to college?"

"You tell me," she prompted. "Do you remember anything about college?"

He gave it a beat, two. Nothing. "Quit playing with me, Grace."

"Okay. I'm just testing your memory. Despite the hacking incident, you earned a scholarship to Berkeley. You attended for two years. You created your first game there. And it was all up-hill from there. As Doug said, you made your first million by the age of twenty-two and your first billion when you were twenty-seven. You own companies and/or properties in fifteen countries. Your net worth is in excess of ten billion. You were *Look* magazine's Man of the Year and *People*'s Sexiest Man Alive the year you made your first billion."

"Very thorough. No wife?"

"No wife. No kids. You were right about that. You're a bit of a player. You've been connected with actresses, models, high-powered executives.

Mostly short-term. You have a couple of long-term relationships." She arched one black eyebrow. "If you consider a year long-term."

He lifted one shoulder in a half shrug. "Sounds like I have commitment issues. With my childhood and bankroll, can you blame me?"

"We all have to grow up sometime. And love has to do with trust not your bank account."

"Says the woman who's never been married. How many long-term relationships have you had?" His life was an open book, or more precisely an open file, to her. Turnabout was fair play.

Her pretty lips pursed as she contemplated him. "Three," she finally answered. "If you consider a year long-term."

He laughed. "Gotcha."

"We're talking about you, not me."

"I'm sounding like a sad character. Properties all over the world but no home. Replaceable women. I hope I have good friends."

"I don't know about that, but I did an internet search, and you have a lot of influential acquaintances."

"That's reassuring." The sarcastic comment slipped out. He tried hard not to whine. But the whole situation tore at his patience.

"Sorry."

He shrugged. "Not your fault. Anything about the people I work with?"

"You have four people in your top echelon. Your legal counsel, Ryan Green. Financial advisor, Jethro Calder. And security executive, Clay Hoffman. The three of them go back to your foster days with you. Your associate Sierra Ross is a Harvard attorney. I've just started looking into them. I'll have more tomorrow."

"Good." He finished his wine and asked, "What about the stabbing? You haven't mentioned that."

"Are you sure you want to hear this tonight? We can go over it tomorrow, when you're more rested."

"I want to hear it now."

"Okay. Well, according to the report, you stated a woman you were dating went wacko when you refused to let her spend the night. Her name is Vanessa Miller. She began by throwing things at you, and when you tried to restrain her, she stabbed you with a piece of broken metal frame. Sometime during the altercation, you were able to activate a panic button. She slipped away while security was seeing to you."

"A real winner. I guess I can really pick them." Every word she spoke drilled a nail into his skull.

"Don't judge yourself too harshly." She gave him an out, sympathy strong in her voice. "Dating is a difficult prospect these days. I imagine it's even more so for a man in your position."

He imagined so, too. Truly, how could he know for certain if his date was into him or his money?

"Have the police apprehended her?"

"No. They suggested you beef up your security. Instead, you decided to take a vacation. You took your Harley and went off the grid. That was three weeks ago. Does any of this strike a chord with you?"

Pain streaked down his neck when he shook his head. "It's like hearing a story that happened to someone else. But if the throbbing in my head is anything to go by, it's dead-on."

"Are you okay?" She leaned forward to study his eyes. "Do you want to head back to the room?"

A glare sent her back into her seat.

"I'm just saying I'm ready when you are."

"You need dessert," he insisted. He wouldn't be the reason her meal was cut short. She deserved this treat for all she'd done for him.

"I don't want dessert."

"All women want dessert. Order some anyway."

Blue eyes narrowed on him. "First of all, I'm not all women. Second, I couldn't even finish my steak. We can leave now."

"I'm fine. And I saw you drooling over the chocolate mousse cake when you were looking at the menu. You know you want some."

As if summoned, the waiter appeared. "May I get you anything else tonight?"

"The lady would like dessert." Jackson answered before Grace could send the man away.

Her eyes flashed with annoyance but she smiled at the waiter. "I'll take a piece of the chocolate mousse cake." She turned her saccharine sweet smile on Jackson. "To go, please."

Leave it to her to find a way around him. Fine with him. He'd been staying for her anyway. The waiter quickly returned with the boxed dessert and the bill. Jackson charged it to his room.

In the elevator on the way to the suite Grace dropped a bomb. "Here's something you need to know. A few years ago you started a foundation for displaced teenagers. They're having a big fund-raiser three days from now. You're scheduled to be there, and from all accounts it's something that's pretty important to you."

"I guess that starts our clock ticking then, doesn't it?" Hearing about his childhood, he was proud of the fact he'd also created a way to help. Which meant facing the world whether he had his memory back or not.

"I'll make sure you're ready," she promised.

He keyed them into the suite. Inside, a handful of pink message slips had been placed on the foyer table. He picked them up and waved them for her to see. "I hope you're right, because ready or not, the world has found us."

CHAPTER NINE

SHE TOOK THE pink message slips from him and returned them to the table. "These can wait until tomorrow. I'm ready for our game. Prepare to go down."

Over the past hour she'd seen how rehashing his past had aged him before her eyes. Pain etched lines around his eyes and a clenched jaw drew tendons tight in his neck. The world may be knocking on the door, but it could wait until tomorrow. Tonight he needed to relax. Whether he liked to admit it or not, he was still healing.

"Now, that's just crazy talk." The tension visibly drained from his shoulders. "Nobody beats the master." Without glancing at the messages he headed for the game room.

"I don't know." She trailed behind him, pretending she didn't notice the nice fit of his dress pants over his firm posterior. "The master is broken. I think I've got a shot."

He stopped suddenly and swung around. Her

reflexes were excellent and she stopped short of running into him, but they were still nose to chin. The predatory light in his eyes rooted her to her spot. She could show no weakness.

"Your trash talk won't get to me. I'm not broken, I'm memory-challenged."

She groaned.

"Hey, my instincts and reflexes are as sharp as ever. I've got this."

"Yeah, you keep telling yourself that," she tossed back. He seemed to thrive on the competition. "Just know there will be no mercy when you start whining that you have a concussion." She slid past him, deliberately knocking his shoulder with hers. "I'm going to change. I want to be comfortable when I kick your butt."

"Hmm," he mused, "probably for the best. You'd only distract me in that getup."

"Nice try." She exaggerated the sway of her hips, smiled when she heard him groan. "Five minutes, Hawke. Don't go to sleep on me."

"Babe, I'll be warming up your seat."

In her room she wasted no time kicking off her heels and trading out the dress for jeans and a comfortable sweater. After pulling on a pair of soft socks, she strolled down the hall to claim her seat.

"You're a hoot, Hawke." With her hands on her hips, she stared down at the deep candleholder with three flames flickering merrily about. "This is how it's going to be?"

"I promised you a warm seat." He slouched in his seat, his hands on the control.

"Very funny." She moved the candleholder to the credenza where the reflection of the flames danced on the wall and then dropped down beside him. Scrolling through the avatars, she chose her favorite, a shaggy-haired redhead with more muscles than curves who went by Ruby.

The big screen was split into two separate viewing areas. In "Unleashed," the characters have been dropped in a remote part of the Amazon to be hunted as live prey. The player can save himself if he reaches civilization in the form of the Amazonia Resort and Conservation Range near the origination of the Amazon River in Peru. Many routes ended in dead ends or insurmountable dangers. If the hunters didn't get you, the environment probably would.

She and Jackson would be playing the same game but running their own course. They could

well run into each other in a kill-or-be-killed scenario. They each started with three lives and two
weapons of their choice. She went with a nine
millimeter and a machete. Jackson had a fishing
knife and a crossbow. She noticed both were silent weapons.

"Okay, here are the rules, we'll play nine levels."

"Nine." He muttered a curse under his breath.
"That's a tease."

"We're not going for a marathon here. I just explained I have work yet to do tonight. So, whoever has the most points at each level wins that
level. Whoever wins the most levels wins the
game."

"No way. Speed is an element of the game. I
don't want to be twiddling my thumbs while you
wander about collecting points. Whoever finishes
level nine first is the winner."

"Okay, you're on. First to finish nine wins."
It wouldn't change how she played. Rushing is
what lost the game for most players. "Man up,
Hawke, we're wasting time. I have searches running on your entourage. I want to do an initial
read-through tonight."

"I have my choice." He flicked his thumb and

a tall wiry kid, who looked a lot like Where's Waldo? minus the hat, emerged from the shadows.

"Slippery Syd? You're kidding me. I thought for sure you'd choose one of the muscle-bound behemoths."

"A common mistake many players make. This guy is tough, smart and versatile."

She eyed his profile as he set up the game. "So you do remember how to play."

He sent her a sidelong glance. "I was born knowing."

"Bragging does not equal skill." Squirming in her seat she got set for the go. "I can promise I'll make you work for it."

"Babe," he said, as the game started, "I won't break a sweat."

"Honey, you're going to crash and burn."

At least she hoped so. He kept discounting his concussion, but she counted on it, both to slow down his reflexes and his cunning. She had skills—a girl had to do something to fill the long nights—but he was Jackson Hawke. Her bravado was all bluff.

This may not meet the definition of rest his doctor would recommend, but in her opinion it was better than letting him brood on what was missing in his head or on what he faced in returning to his life without his memories. Playing may require him to use his brain, but it wasn't the part that caused pain every time he had a thought that challenged the block in his head.

Playing relaxed and energized him. Winning would give him confidence to face his friends and associates. Not that she'd let him win. Her avatar slid past a coiled snake, snagged the knapsack that would garner her fifty points and hopefully some ammo and rappelled out of the pit.

She'd disciplined herself to use his real name earlier, for her benefit, but also for his. He needed to get used to hearing and reacting to the name. That's also why she'd switched to his last name to razz him about the game.

Out of the corner of her eyes she saw Slippery Syd taking on an anaconda in level three. Good luck, pal.

If she could get past the sleeping jaguar to get the first aid box on the other side of him, she'd have enough points to advance to level three, as well. One wrong move and she'd be back at the start of level two. She went up and then, by hopping from rock to rock, made it past the napping cat to snag her prize and move up in the game.

While the game reset her at level three, she shook her hands and flexed her fingers.

"Congratulations," Hawke taunted, "you're only half a level behind."

"A quarter level," she corrected. "And that can change in a heartbeat."

As she spoke, he missed his footing on a jump and landed in the river. Piranhas were on him in an instant and he lost his first life.

"Poor Slippery Syd. Now we're even again." Her level three started and she had a plan. There was antivenom on this level she may need later. She'd make for that before Hawke could get there and then advance straight to level four.

As the game went on, they continued to jab good-naturedly at each other. He combined quick wit and easy flirting to make her laugh. She kept striking at his ego, but it had little effect. Her barbs bounced off his thick hide.

No doubt she could distract him by responding to his flirtation. But uh-uh. They'd already been down that road, and she wasn't encouraging him. Her sanity and ability to do her job depended on her restraint.

But, oh, how he tempted her.

He was funny and quick. And he smelled good. Such a distraction.

He reached the ninth level right ahead of her and they were both down to their last lives. She decided to forgo any attempt at points or resources to go straight for the finish line.

She chanced a quick look at his screen and determined he'd made the same decision. Dang, he must have muscle memory for this game because he seemed to know right where to go.

Don't rush, she cautioned herself. *Sure and steady will win this game.*

Stealth was needed on this level as the hunters were close. At one point she saw Slippery Syd ahead of her on the path to the waterfall. If he continued straight, he'd get to the top faster than her, but he'd be exposed. She chose to go farther down the river, under cover of the foliage. The ascent was less severe but longer.

She had to hope he made a mistake.

Because she was watching him reach the waterfall summit, she walked right into a hunter. He had his sights on Slippery Syd, but when she stumbled into the clearing, he immediately turned his gun on her. Ruby dove to the ground expecting the kill shot. Instead there was a thump. She slowly lifted her head to see a bow bolt had taken out the hunter. Slippery Syd had saved her.

And he'd also won. Except a shot rang out, echoing on both screens. And Slippery Syd fell, his last life taken by a hunter. Because he'd re- vealed his position to save her.

Next to her, Hawke cursed.

No fair. He'd had the win. She made a mad dash and wild jump, windmilling her arms and legs in an attempt to reach a ledge on the rock face of the waterfall. Ruby missed and fell, suf- fering the same fate as Slippery Syd.

"You didn't have to do that." Jackson admon- ished her.

"I kind of did." She assured him. "The win is yours."

"You had more points."

"And you reached more levels faster."

"I'm not claiming a game I didn't win."

"Fine, we'll call it a draw." She tucked her con- trol pad into the sleeve on the front of her seat. "I look forward to the rematch." His insistence said a lot about his sense of fair play. One more thing to admire about the man, when there were already so many.

"I'm ready if you are." His slumberous gaze rolled over her, suggesting he was ready for more than a friendly game.

She licked her lips, suddenly wishing he was just JD, someone in her sphere she might actually have a chance at having a relationship with, someone who might stick around and build a home with her. From the number of stamps in his passport, Jackson was a jet-setter. Out of her reach and out of her league.

"Oh, no." She rose and backed away. "Shall we say tomorrow night, same time, same place? Ah…I…uh, have some reading to do. I'll see you at breakfast."

Whipping around, she fled temptation.

Grace jerked awake. Something had broken her sleep, but what? She'd left her door ajar an inch or two in case Jackson called out. Was that what woke her? Was he in distress? She sat up.

Then she heard it, a hoarse call sounded from down the hall.

Jackson!

She pushed the covers aside and, not worrying over the fact she wore only an oversize white T-shirt and Tweety pajama shorts, she raced down the hall.

Another shout.

She reached his door and found it slightly open, but by less than an inch. Knocking, she called out, "Jackson? Are you okay?" She waited a beat and then repeated, "Jackson?"

A low moan leaked through the crack in the door. Waiting no longer, she knocked again and pushed into the room. A three-inch swath of light from the bathroom illuminated the room.

"Jackson." He sat up in bed, bare to the waist where the covers pooled around him. He slumped forward, head cradled in his hands. She sat on the edge of the bed and placed her hand on his blanket-covered thigh. She realized he was shaking. "What is it? Do you need a pain pill? Or a doctor?"

"No." And more emphatically, "No." But he didn't release his head. He cursed. "I'm fine. You can go back to bed."

"I don't think so. Tell me what's going on."

"Nothing. Stupid nightmare." He groaned through gritted teeth. "Maybe I will take a pain pill." He reached for a bottle on the nightstand.

"I'll get you some water." She went to the bathroom and returned with a glass of water. He took the pill and she placed the bottle and glass on the bedside table. "Tell me about the dream."

He rolled one bare shoulder. "It's gone. Go to bed. I'm sorry I woke you."

Ignoring him, she reclaimed her spot on the bed, curling one leg up under her. Men were such babies when it came to being in pain, physical or mental. And dealing with them was much the same as dealing with an infant. You knew something was wrong, but it was up to you to figure out what.

"I've heard it's good to talk about a nightmare right after. It's supposed to help release its grip on you."

He laid his hand on top of hers on his leg. Only then did she realize she'd been petting him. "Fair warning, if you don't leave my room, I'm going to get a grip on you."

Knowing he meant the sexual threat to chase her away, she dismissed the warning. The medicine would help, but he was in no shape to make love. "I'm not worried. I'm pretty sure I could knock you down with a feather."

"Babe," he drawled, his voice low and sleep-roughened, "it would be a mistake to equate down with out."

Okay. A shiver of awareness rolled down her spine.

"When you say gone, do you mean the dream is over and done or you don't remember the dream?"

"Does it matter?"

"No," she acknowledged, watching him closely. At least the shaking had eased under the hand he held to his thigh. Evidence the pain pill was working. Good. "I imagine it would be disconcerting either way."

"All I remember is being stabbed and then waking up to crushing pain in my head."

"Interesting. Perhaps it wasn't a dream, but a memory. Maybe that's why your head hurts. You said that happens when a memory tries to come through."

"Maybe."

Seriously? Could he be more stubborn? "Did you get a sense of the woman at all? I'd really like to have more than a driver's license picture to go on as we get ready to head to Las Vegas."

"I'm with you on that." He ran his thumb over the back of her hand. "One of the first things I want to do is go in and talk to the detectives, get an update on where things stand."

"Good idea." He'd already mentioned his desire for more information. But the heat in his eyes told her his mind had shifted away from the conversation to more basic functions. Maybe he wasn't as debilitated as she thought. Time to go.

"Ah, you look like you could sleep now." She tried to ease her hand away from him. "I'll just go."

His hand tightened on hers and she tensed. Then he released her and she thought for a moment she was free. But in one quick move he circled her waist in his big hands, pulled her up and over him and then turned so she was under him. In the space of a few seconds she went from sitting on the edge of the bed to blinking up at a man with wicked intentions on his mind.

"So, Delaney, where is this feather you were talking about?"

His molten gaze rolled over her curves, touching on the skin where her shirt had ridden up at the waist, lingered on the dark shadow of nipple under white cloth and traced the flow of shoulder into neck exposed by the stretch of her collar.

"Huh?" She dragged in a much-needed breath.

Sweet potatoes and pecan pie, she was in so much trouble. If just the feel of his eyes set her on fire, what would happen when he actually used his hands on her?

She couldn't risk finding out.

"Okay," she said, wincing because it was more of an aroused croak, "I get the message." She wiggled to the right, gained a few inches of space. "I'll see you in the morning."

"Uh-uh." He dragged her back and hooked a leg over hers to keep her from squirming away. "I gave you your chance to get away." He buried his nose in her hair, and moaned softly. She almost echoed the sound. He smelled so good, of citrus and spice and a touch of woodiness that made her mouth water. "You didn't take it, which tells me you are right where you want to be."

"We really shouldn't do this." His hand landed on her stomach right where the shirt left her bare. Pure instinct had her arching into his touch. Still, she fought for reason. "I'm listening now. I'll go."

"Too late." The heat of his breath on her throat sent a shiver racing through her. "I take my threats seriously. Unlike you, since there is no feather to knock me away with. Ah, the things I could do to you with that feather."

To demonstrate he trailed his fingers, feather-light on the cotton of her shirt, up her torso, along the side of her breast, over her collarbone, where skin met skin and she lost her battle to contain a moan. When he reached her neck, he flipped his hand to use the back of his fingers to lift her chin to the perfect angle to receive his kiss.

Oh, so soft, his mouth settled on hers. She opened for him instantly. His tongue met hers in a dance of wonder. Not a passionate tango, but a slow waltz of turns and holds and the occasional lunge. She sighed and went boneless beneath him.

"Stop," she pleaded. No matter how good this felt, she worked for him. "You have to stop."

"Careful." He nipped her chin with his teeth. "Or I will."

"Oh, you're evil."

"Because I insist you admit you want me as much as I want you?" He fondled the lobe of her ear with his tongue. Her entire lower body tightened. "Or because I don't agree we need to keep business and personal separated? Yes, I'm a bad, bad man."

His hand went to the bottom of her T-shirt, and

bunching it, he pushed the fabric upward. Looking her in the eye, he demanded, "Yes or no?"

She knew what she should say, what her dad had taught her, what her career and all her training warranted. Yet never had she yearned for a man more. His strength tempered by his vulnerability got to her on a visceral level. Arching into him as he drew her closer, her eyes fell shut on a sigh.

"Yes. Oh, please, yes."

She expected her clothes to disappear, for him to jump on her offer. And her. Which, oh yeah, she was more than ready for. Instead, he leaned down and soft lips opened over hers. His tongue sought hers and now they tangoed. He led with authority, a true aficionado who seduced with desire and demand. Senses dazzled, she followed every synchronized twist and slow, passionate pivot, sinking into the bedding and drawing him to her.

Her clothes did disappear somewhere along the line, and she reveled in his touch on her flesh. She fought past blankets to reach him, to rid him of whatever he wore, only to find smooth, unencumbered skin. Oh, my. Long and lean, he was beautiful, marred only by the nearly healed wound on his abdomen. Her fingers went to the scar.

"Learning the details of what happened probably sparked your nightmare. Won't you talk to me?"

He was silent for a beat then he sighed. "I can't recall much, mostly emotions—confusion, anger, shock. It gives me a massive headache to think about it," he stated dismissively. His fingers closed over hers, pulling her hand away from the scar. "Does it offend you?"

Surprised by the question, she blinked up at him. In the shifting of his gaze she saw the geek lurking behind the stud. "No." She squeezed his hand and then freed herself to caress the scar with her thumb. "I was a master-at-arms in the navy. I've seen much worse. But that doesn't mean it's not still raw. It won't hurt you to make love?"

He grinned, confidence fully restored. "Babe, my head bothers me more than that little cut. Fortunately, you gave me a pain pill. I'm primed and ready to go, and I can't think of a better way than in your arms. Such a sweet armful. I may have no memory, but I know spectacular when I'm curled up next to her in bed."

Ah, so smooth and yet her heart still melted.

"Still wishing I had a feather, though."

"Would you forget the feather?"

"Not going to happen," he assured her. "I'll just have to improvise some more." He continued to tease her, drawing a single finger between the valley of her breasts and then to a peak, where the light touch tormented her into arching into his touch, demanding more.

Instead he shifted his attention, moving his imaginary feather lower.

"Stop," she said around a giggle, grabbing his hand at her waist. "Well, we've learned you aren't inhibited."

"I'd say not, as I consider feather play to be quite tame."

Have mercy. It made the mind boggle at what he would find to be kinky.

He nuzzled her neck, using his tongue to dampen her skin, and then blew gently in a new form of sensual teasing. The shift from the heat of his mouth to the cool of his breath brought goose bumps to her skin and the desire to get closer. She bowed her neck, giving him better access.

"And you are quite skilled."

She felt him grin against her skin. "So happy you're pleased."

"Oh, I am. But I have to wonder." She moved her hands around from his back and trailed her thumbs slowly, oh, so slow, down his sides. "Are you ticklish?"

"Let's not find out." He bucked up, grabbed her hands in both of his, anchored them to the bed and took her mouth again, slowly lowering himself onto her, linking them in the ultimate dance. Where thought surrendered to sensation and bodies communicated without words.

No longer teasing, he twirled her between moments of utter tenderness, when she felt cherished and special, to sweeps of passionate intensity that drew the wanton out of her. Oh, yeah, she liked that, liked demanding he please her, liked hearing his groans when she pleased him.

Touch for touch, kiss for kiss, her heart raced to the beat of his as pleasure spiraled past excitement and joy to euphoria. And she clung to him as they both plunged into bliss.

Grace curled up in Jackson's arms. Her life had changed forever. She loved him. Crazy, of course. She was a former public servant and he was a billionaire. She wanted to put down roots and he lived in hotels. She craved order and he created games that thrived on chaos.

There was no future for them. She accepted that, but she could have now. She could have his back and make sure he got the rest he needed to heal. And grab every moment possible with him before he got his memory back and didn't need her anymore.

She had her head on straight when she met Jackson in the first-floor restaurant for breakfast. She admired the French-bistro vibe as she ordered fresh fruit and a croissant. Between bites of strawberries and buttery, flaky bread she filled him in on his senior staff.

"They're quite an impressive bunch." He flipped through the reports she'd given him. He still couldn't read well, but there were pictures so he could put faces to names.

"You're pretty impressive, too." She handed him her last packet, a file on him he could read when his vision improved. "You have to remember you're not working at your normal speed. When I had a concussion, it took me four weeks to feel right again. I know people where it took months."

"So you keep saying."

"Because you're expecting too much from yourself too soon."

He pushed his plate of unfinished eggs aside. "I don't have a choice, do I? Two days from now I have to be back in Las Vegas to face a room full of people as a man I have no idea how to portray."

"Actually, sooner than that." She faced the front of the restaurant and over his shoulder she saw two men approaching. "Bogies at six o'clock. Jethro Calder and Clay Hoffman are headed this way. That's your financial advisor and your head of security."

Both men were tall, dark and handsome. Not exactly a cliché she could rattle off to Jackson. The executives were about the same height—easily six feet, maybe an inch or two over—and wore expensive business suits. Jethro Calder wore navy blue with a pin-striped tie. He had short black hair and his picture failed to show the depth of his blue eyes. Clay Hoffman carried more weight, in the form of muscle mass, and wore black on black with no tie. His hair and eyes were dark chocolate-brown.

Both were larger-than-life characters, confident, assertive, intimidating. And Jackson put them both to shame.

"Maybe we should have responded to those message slips, after all."

"And said what? Jackson can't come to the phone right now because he doesn't remember who you are?" He chugged a sip of coffee as if it was a bracing shot of fine whiskey. "I'll handle this."

"Jackson," Jethro Calder greeted him as the two men arrived at the table. "You're a hard man to get a hold of." He felt comfortable enough with the boss to pull out a chair and join them at the table for four.

Clay was more direct as he took his seat. "What the hell, Hawke? You can't go off the grid without letting me know. I've had men looking for you for the past two days." His dark gaze narrowed in on Jackson's jaw. "Is that a bruise?"

"I knew this trip was a bad idea," Jethro tossed in. He grasped Jackson's chin to turn his head for a better view of the bruise. "What happened to you?"

Jackson pulled away and held up a staying hand. "First of all, Grace, these Neanderthals work for me. Jethro Calder and Clay Hoffman, this is Grace Delaney."

Two assessing gazes landed on her.

"Ma'am." Clay nodded at her, his dark eyes already having cataloged everything about her, from her shoe size to her short crop of hair. "How long have you and Jackson been friends?"

"Not long," she assured him. She'd only brought her wallet downstairs. She pulled out an old business card, flipped it over and wrote her social security number on it before calmly handing it to him.

"You don't have to do that, Grace," Jackson's protest had a bite to it. He nailed his men with an intent stare. "She's with me. That's all you need to know."

"I have nothing to hide," she soothed him. "He'll check me out anyway. This just makes it easier for everyone."

"Sheriff of Woodpark?" Clay mused.

"Ex-sheriff, actually. My term ended on the thirty-first."

"Hmm." He tucked her card into his pocket as he turned back to Jackson. "Tell us about the bruise."

Jackson simply lifted one dark eyebrow.

The security exec didn't back down. He rolled his impressive shoulders and pinned Jackson to his chair with an intense stare. "Protecting you is my job. I can't do that when you take off on your own. I need to know what happened to determine if you need additional medical care."

"He does," Grace said.

"I don't." Jackson sent her an admonishing glare.

The two men looked back and forth between them.

"Which is it?" Jethro asked.

"He has a severe concussion. And he left the hospital against the doctor's recommendation." Her gaze never left Jackson's during her revelation so she saw the flash of hurt quickly replaced by irritation.

"You're supposed to be on my side."

"Always." She made it a promise. "Which is why your health comes first. He's handling himself." She flicked her gaze to Clay. "But he should definitely see his physician when he returns to Las Vegas."

"Maybe you need to start from the beginning." Clay directed the comment to his boss.

Jackson sighed. Showing his aggravation, he

crossed his arms over his chest. "As she said, I have a concussion. Our best bet is someone ran me off the road and stole my wallet and my motorcycle. I don't remember much about the incident."

Grace hid her surprise. She hadn't expected him to be so forthcoming.

"An officer took me to the sheriff's office, where I met Grace. She's been an angel."

He ran a finger over the back of her hand on the table. Dang the man. The deliberate gesture was obviously meant to solidify the impression they were a couple. She narrowed her eyes in a what-the-heck look and he moved his head in a sideways just-go-with-it gesture. She didn't like where this was going, but she left her hand where it was.

"She went with me to the hospital and then drove me to Santa Rosa for more tests. And, no, I didn't want to stay overnight for a pounding head. You know how I am about hospitals."

"Concussions can be dangerous."

Uh-huh. Grace applauded Clay's warning. Vindicated at last. Perhaps his associate could actually get Jackson back to the doctor. She'd caught on to his game. He was giving them just enough truth to placate them without revealing the true extent of his injuries.

"Believe me, Grace isn't letting me overexert myself."

"Does the sheriff's department have any leads on your motorcycle?" Jethro asked.

"Not as of yesterday." Graced fielded the question. "It would be helpful if someone could forward the license and vehicle identification numbers to the sheriff's office. Jackson was a little slim on details."

"A concussion can mess with short-term memory." Clay played right into Jackson's version of events.

"What brings you two here?" Jackson changed the subject. "Any fires I need to know about?"

"No. We have things covered," Jethro assured him. "Development is eager to have your input on the new game, but mostly we were concerned at not hearing from you for nearly a week. Especially after recent events."

"So they haven't apprehended Vanessa yet?"

Jethro glanced at Grace before answering. "No."

Jackson gave a grim nod. "Sorry to give you a

scare. I guess with this head thing I forgot it had been so long since I checked in."

"Yeah." Clay leaned back in his chair. "I can see you've been distracted. We have the corporate jet. Do you want to catch a ride with us back to Las Vegas?"

"No."

"Jackson." Both men spoke at the same time.

He shrugged. "I want another day with Grace."

"I think we should go," Grace inserted. Jackson scowled, but she nodded subtly. "Your people need you. It's time for us to join the real world. It had to happen sometime." Grr. She turned her hand over and threaded their fingers together. "We'll still be together."

His fingers tightened on hers. "You heard the lady. I guess we're headed home to Las Vegas."

CHAPTER TEN

GRACE HIGHLY RECOMMENDED flying by private luxury jet. The one they traveled on had a seating area—better than the normal first class—a living room area, with a big-screen TV and wet bar, and a bedroom area. Both bathrooms had small showers. The appointments were luxurious, the seating comfortable.

The flight took less than two hours. And then she and the three men were in a limousine headed for the Las Vegas Pinnacle Hotel, the showpiece of the Pinnacle properties.

Her jaw dropped as she walked hand in hand through the lobby with Jackson. Just like San Francisco the hotel followed the theme of the game, but to a much larger degree. She felt as if she'd walked into a city wrestled from the desolation of the apocalypse and jazzed up as only Vegas could do.

"This is too cool." Jackson leaned down to

whisper in her ear. "I want to shake these guys and explore."

Jethro and Clay walked ahead of them, leading them to the elevators.

"I want to shake these guys and talk." She held up their joined hands and nodded to them significantly. They hadn't been alone since breakfast. His executives joined them in the suite while they packed up and then they'd been on the road.

"We will," he assured her.

Clay walked past the bank of hotel elevators, turned right and pushed through a door marked Private. Down a short hall was a bank of service elevators. He stopped in front of the first one and used a keycard to activate the call button.

"I called ahead and requested a new set of keys for you. Since you lost your wallet, we recoded all the locks just to be on the safe side. Sierra will have yours upstairs." The elevator arrived and he used the keycard again to access the penthouse level.

"So Jackson has a secret elevator?" Grace asked. "How covert."

Clay looked down his nose at her. "It's a matter of security."

"Because of the woman who stabbed him?"

He lifted a dark eyebrow, showing his surprise that Jackson had confided in her about the attack. "She's a good example of why precautions are necessary."

"Ms. Delaney," Jethro cut in. "Once we reach the penthouse, Jackson's associate will escort you to your room. We have to catch him up on business matters."

"She'll be staying with me," Jackson declared.

Shock rolled across Jethro's face. He sent a questioning glance Clay's way. Trained to show no emotion, Clay masked his reaction. Their surprise was quite telling. Obviously Jackson didn't normally allow his companions to stay with him in his suite. He really did hold himself apart.

No wonder the two men didn't know what to make of her. She didn't fit in his world and he wasn't acting himself. Tension tightened through her shoulders. All her arguments against putting on a false romantic front just took a hit. If they wanted to avoid suspicion, Jackson's pretense of a relationship was their best bet.

People did crazy things when they were in love. His uncharacteristic behavior would make his staff all the more suspicious of her, which gave them the added bonus of switching their focus from Jackson to her.

Uh-huh. Just because it was a brilliant strategy didn't mean she'd let him get away with launching it without talking to her first.

The hotel suite matched the owner's suite in San Francisco. She imagined in everyday life the familiarity gave Jackson a false sense of home-coming. In these unusual circumstances, it helped with his charade.

She led the way into the living room and a spectacular view of the Las Vegas strip opened up before her. The hotel rooms resembled each other, but the views were singular. No pretending you were in the same place when the view was on display.

Then again, a push of a button could fix that problem.

A slim blonde in a chic navy dress and an older gentleman, round in the middle and bald on top, waited in the living room. Jethro took care of introductions.

"Grace, this is Sierra Ross, Jackson's personal assistant. And Dr. Wilcox, his personal physician. Sierra, Doctor, this is Jackson's new friend, Grace Delaney."

"Hello." To cover Jackson's sudden tension, Grace broke away to shake hands. "Dr. Wilcox, I'm glad to see you, though I'm sure you know Jackson isn't."

The man laughed and patted her hand before releasing it. "Oh, I'm aware I'm not his favorite person. A necessary evil at best. But he sends me a stellar bottle of brandy for Christmas every year, so it's a trade-off."

"Don't be upset, Jackson." Sierra brought her brooding boss into the conversation. "Clay mentioned you had a concussion and that Grace recommended you see Dr. Wilcox. I thought it best to bring him here."

"It's fine." Jackson strolled forward and held out his hand. "Thank you for coming, Doc. Do you mind if we get this over with?"

"No problem." The doctor patted his arm after shaking hands. "Shall we go to your room?"

"That works." Jackson came to her. "You'll be all right on your own?" He kissed her on the temple. Up close his displeasure seared her. He whispered, "When I'm done, we need to talk."

"Yes, we do." She lovingly ran her hand down his chest while talking through gritted teeth. "Do yourself a favor, be frank with the doctor. You might be surprised at how he can help you."

"Do you want to come with me?"

"No. You're a big boy. And I agree with your first instinct. These guys would find it odd if I joined you. It's obvious you don't let women get too close."

"Yeah, well, the last one I dated stabbed me. And come to think of it, you're probably armed."

She didn't respond and his eyes went wide.

"You are armed, aren't you?"

"Shh. Not at this moment. But yes, I own a gun. If your man hasn't confiscated it."

"I should have known." Anxiety clouded his gaze. "I'm supposed to be a genius, and it doesn't occur to me that a woman who is ex-military, ex-sheriff would carry a gun."

"It's the concussion." She brushed the hair from his eyes, watched heat push back the anxiety. "Talk to the doctor. Let him help you."

He sighed. "Okay. But it's going to cost you." And he kissed her. In front of everyone. His mouth covered hers in a soft claiming. It lasted only a moment. A hot, sensual moment that stole her breath and had her hooking an arm around his neck to get closer, to extend the caress that ended way too soon.

No, the kiss didn't last long, but the power of it reached all the way to her tingling toes. She slowly opened her eyes to find him smiling down at her.

"These guys are smart. It has to look real to fool them."

Grace sank back on her heels. "Oh, your strategy is working. All too well." Best she remember it was all for show. "Go away now."

He left with the doctor and she found herself alone with his cohorts. Pretending a confidence she only half felt, she chose a chair and sat.

"Would you care for some coffee?" Sierra rose from the futuristic sofa as she made her way to the bar where a carafe and cups were situated. "I must say I've never seen Jackson so attentive."

Before Grace could respond to the leading comment, the suite door opened and a man walked in. Sweet merciful angels, he was gorgeous. Of mixed heritage, he had light brown skin and dreamy gold eyes. He wore his black hair skull close.

"Sorry I'm late." He stopped in front of her. "You must be Grace."

His eyes weren't so dreamy now. They raked over her, assessing every little detail. Jackson's chief counsel made no secret he questioned her presence here.

"And you must be Ryan. Nice to meet you."

"Really? Has Jackson told you a lot about me?" He spread his arms wide, asking, "About us? We can't say the same about you."

"Oh. Well, our relationship is still very new." She gave a half shrug. "Don't blame him. He's not totally himself at the moment."

"Exactly." Jethro jumped on her response. "So you can understand our concern that he's taken up with a stranger."

"I would think you'd be happy he had someone to help him in a moment of dire need. Or is your concern only of a professional nature? Is Jackson simply your boss, or do any of you look on him as a friend?"

The room bristled with hostility.

Clay surged to his feet. "We've been a team for ten years. You have no right to question our loyalty to him."

She relaxed as the others nodded, confirming his impassioned declaration. "Good. Then we all have Jackson's best interests at heart."

"Do we?"

"Ryan, gentlemen, why don't you all have a seat?" Sierra suggested as she poured two cups of coffee—one black, one with two sugars. "And Grace can tell us more about herself."

The men sat, all of them perching on the edge of their chosen seat. All focused their attention on her.

Great. She'd always longed to have the undivided attention of three of the most powerful men in corporate America.

Not.

Yet here she was. Nothing for her to do but bluster her way through it.

"You mean in addition to what you've all read in the report Clay had done before we ever touched ground in Las Vegas?" She met each person's gaze straight on. She had nothing to hide. The secrets were Jackson's, not hers. "I think you all have a fair idea of who I am."

Sierra joined them in the living area. She handed one cup of coffee to Ryan and kept the other.

"You grew up a navy brat. Speak four foreign languages—French, German, Italian and Japanese."

"Are they really foreign if you live there?" she asked rhetorically.

"Joined the navy at the age of seventeen with your father's permission. Your military record is clean. You received several commendations and were accelerating well through the ranks until you quit to care for your ailing father, a retired Senior Chief Petty Officer." Jethro ran through her history as if reading a list. Probably because he had. "Finished your father's term as sheriff in Woodpark when he passed. Ran for sheriff yourself but lost."

"Why is that, Grace?" Clay demanded. "What did you do to upset the good citizens of Woodpark?"

Being it was a question she'd asked herself more than once, the query threw Grace as her confidence took a hit. He knew right where to strike to make her question herself. But she quickly regrouped. She'd done her best for the people of Woodpark. It wasn't her skills that had been in question.

Now she inhaled a deep breath, fought back her insecurities and projected a calm she didn't feel to attempt to put them at ease.

"I did my job." The point wasn't to sell herself

to them, but to let them know she wasn't a threat to Jackson. She crossed her legs. "But that's not what you really care about is it? What you really want to know is what my intentions are regarding your boss. The answer is I have none."

"None." Ryan infused the word with skepticism.

"None," she confirmed. She ran a finger down the crease in her jeans. "Look, we met under unusual circumstances, which caused us to bond quickly. At first I didn't know who he really was. He needed help and I was happy to put Woodpark in my rearview mirror. Bottom line, we all agree he's not his usual self. I don't expect our relationship to last past his full recovery. But it's not every day a girl gets romanced by a billionaire. I'm just enjoying the time we have together."

She knew immediately it was the right note to strike. The men looked at each other and relaxed back in their seats.

"He has a lot of money." Jethro stated the obvious.

"He does." She left it at that. She had no designs on Jackson's money, but the more she tried to convince this group of that fact, the less credible she'd sound.

"A lot of women lose sight of the man for the money." Clay observed.

"I knew the man first, his money doesn't interest me. But the trappings are fun. I've never flown in a private jet before."

"So we all agree this will be a short-lived affair."

"No." A deep voice stated from the archway near the foyer. Jackson stood there. "We are not in agreement. My relationship with Grace is none of your business. I'll thank you all to stay out of it."

"Jackson," Sierra sought to appease him, saying, "we're only looking out for you."

By the jut of his chin she'd failed. "I don't need you to look out for me. Grace is the last person I, or you, need to worry about. My money is safe from her. Grace." He held out his hand to her, a demand to join him.

She made her way to his side, took his hand. "Don't overreact," she warned him.

"I won't let them intimidate you."

"I can handle myself. These are the people you rely on daily, who will be here for you long after I'm gone from your life."

"You're the one I know. The one who is here for me now. I won't let them hurt you."

"They haven't." Only he had the power to do that.

But that was her problem.

The fact she loved him changed nothing. Yes, having him take her side reinforced that feeling, but as far as this group was concerned their relationship didn't go beyond a fun time. Couldn't go beyond that. She *was* enjoying their time together, and that was all there could ever be between them.

"Hmm." His gaze flicked to his associates, skepticism clear in the green depths. Had he heard more than she thought? A hand in the small of her back urged her through the archway. "Let's go."

"Jackson," Ryan hailed him. "Are you leaving? I wanted to get with you."

"Later. I need to take my lady shopping."

Shopping? Grace hid an inner grimace. She just got this crew on her side and he probably wiped all her hard work out with that one statement. Not to mention, shopping for what?

"I'm not letting you buy me another thing," she muttered for his ears only.

On the other side of him Ryan said, "I thought you'd want to catch up on what we've done while you've been gone."

"Jethro indicated everything was under control." Jackson threaded his fingers through hers. "After what I overheard, I need to spend the next few hours showing Grace I want her here." Jackson released Grace to walk over and hand Sierra his phone. "I lost my old phone in the accident. Can you update all my contacts and then send me the itinerary for the foundation gala?"

"Uh, sure." Sierra looked shell-shocked. As did the men, to a lesser degree.

Jackson came back and reclaimed her hand. As he led her through the archway, he tossed a final comment over his shoulder. "Grace's number is in there. If anyone needs me they can call her number."

Fury fueled Jackson's pace into the elevator and then to the front desk.

"Good afternoon, sir." A young man dressed in the dark blue-and-black hotel colors greeted him.

"Do you know who I am?" Jackson demanded.

The young man's eyes widened as if he'd been presented with a sudden pop quiz. He cleared his throat. "Of course, Mr. Hawke. It's good to have you back with us."

Jackson nodded. "I'd like two keys to the penthouse suite." He drew Grace forward. "This is my guest, Grace Delaney. She is to be treated with respect. Anything she asks for is to be charged to me."

"Of course. Welcome, Ms. Delaney."

"Thank you." Next to Jackson, Grace tensed. She twisted her hand in his seeking freedom.

He held on. He always held on.

"You need to calm down," she murmured softly when the clerk looked away to deal with the keys.

"I'm fine." He seethed with indignation on her behalf. She'd done nothing but help him and those self-satisfied blowhards upstairs treated her like a money-grubbing groupie.

"No, I'm fine," she argued. "*You* are overreacting."

"Don't tell me how to feel." Pain spiked as the high emotions sent the blood pounding through his head. He didn't care. Bring on the hurt. He wouldn't allow Grace to be disrespected. His so-called entourage better get behind the notion real quick or they'd be looking for new jobs real soon.

"Here you go, Mr. Hawke. Is there anything more I can help you with?"

"Thank you, no." With keys in one hand, her hand in the other, he headed back to the elevator and the shops down below but changed his mind halfway there and went for the front door instead. He'd had enough of this fishbowl.

A valet immediately appeared. "Hello, do you have a ticket?"

"No." But Jackson automatically patted his pocket, which reminded him he held the keys. He dropped one in his pocket and handed the other to Grace. "Just bring something around," he said.

"Excuse me, sir," The valet, a man in his late twenties with sideburns and a goatee, protested. "You need a ticket. Or would you like a taxi?"

Great. Just when he counted on his identity to work for him, he gets the one valet who doesn't know who he is.

"Mr. Hawke." The concierge bustled up. His name tag read R. Schultz. "I have this, Pete. What can we do for you, sir?"

Finally. "I have vehicles here, right?"

"Yes, sir." The robust man took the question

in stride. "You have six vehicles housed here in a private section of the garage."

Six? Jackson figured he had something besides a motorcycle, but six? What did he do with six vehicles? Never mind, he didn't even want to think about that.

He nodded for the concierge's benefit. "Have something brought around, would you?"

"No preference, sir? Perhaps the Ferrari or the Hummer?"

"Something simple, please," Grace spoke up. "Mr. Hawke isn't feeling himself this afternoon."

Jackson's neck twitched. He dropped Grace's hand. He didn't care to have his condition advertised to the world. Something he'd let her know once they were alone.

"Of course." Schultz waved Pete over and passed on the request. "Your car will be right here. I hope you feel better soon, sir."

"Thank you." Jackson gave him a generous tip. And when Pete pulled up in a sporty BMW, Jackson tipped him well and prepared to slide behind the wheel.

"Jackson."

Hearing his name, he paused to see Jethro striding toward him. His associate extended a slim leather wallet toward him. "If you're shopping, you'll need these. Sierra had your cards replaced."

Jackson accepted the wallet, nodded and slipped into the driver's seat. He wasted no time putting the car in gear and pulling away from the hotel.

"There was no need to mention my health." He gritted out between clenched teeth as he pulled out on Las Vegas Boulevard known the world over as The Strip.

"I wouldn't have had to if you hadn't looked like you were about to explode." She adjusted the seat belt over her middle. She stared straight out the windshield, her profile perfectly capturing her mood with the proud jut of her chin.

"Someone needs to be upset over how you were being treated. I won't have them disrespecting you."

That brought her head around along with the full force of her ire. "I told you I can handle myself. It may not have looked like it back there, but I won that skirmish, and you wiped it all out with your stupid comment about going shopping."

"Don't call me stupid. I'm a genius, after all." Being a billionaire was hard work, so many elements to juggle. The money was good, but sometimes he wished he could go back to being JD.

"I didn't call you stupid. I said your comment was stupid. There's a difference."

"Not from where I'm sitting." He inched the car along, overshadowed by the marble columns of Caesar's Palace on one side and the Eiffel Tower on the other. "I heard them all but call you a gold digger." He gave her a brief glance. "You're important to me. They're not."

"Yes, they are," she said with exquisite gentleness. "You just don't remember them right now. And yes, they want to protect you. Were they out of line? A little. Was I insulted? No." She waved her hand at him saying, "Billionaire," and then at herself continuing, "Peon. What are they supposed to think?"

"That I can take care of myself. That I have the intelligence to choose a companion I can trust."

There was a beat of silence as she did him the courtesy of not mentioning the woman who stabbed him.

"Okay," he conceded, "so they may have a small reason for concern."

She laughed, a soft chuckle that invited him to

join in the fun. "See, you are a smart man. Please tell me we aren't really going shopping."

"Yes, we are. Unless you have a ball gown tucked away in that duffel bag of yours."

"Uh, no." He felt her studying his profile. "Why would I need a ball gown? Because of the gala? I'm okay. I have the black dress you bought."

"You can't go in the black dress."

"Why not? It's a beautiful dress."

"And you looked beautiful in it. But didn't you see the posters at the hotel? They showed everyone dressed up in monkey suits and long gowns. You might ordinarily get away with wearing the black dress, but you'll be my date so you'll have to wear something spectacular."

"Humph." She settled back in her seat. "The things I do for you. Well, you're not buying it."

"Actually, I am." She could argue all she liked, he was firm on this.

She huffed. "We're not going through this again."

"Nope. Because as you said, you're doing this for me. That means I pay."

"I can afford my own clothes."

"I can afford it more." He sent her a quick, emphatic glance. "Resign yourself, Grace. I'm not letting you pay for anything more while you're helping me. At the very least I can cover your costs."

She stared out her window, tapping on her armrest. "I could point out your friends would then be right about me."

"Come on, Grace, don't do that." He rolled his neck, working on the tension building there.

"Instead I'll ask, why is it so important to you?"

He spotted a billboard advertising a mall in Caesar's and maneuvered a U-turn while he considered how to answer her. Instinctively he sought to protect himself, then he remembered she'd been his advocate before he knew he needed help. She was his one constant since losing his memory.

Bottom line, he trusted her.

He waited to answer until after he left the car with the valet and led her inside the mall.

"I have so little control over anything right now. My memory is shot. I'm supposed to be a genius, yet I feel as though it takes forever to process anything."

She looked ready to protest but he'd heard her argument enough times to know what she'd say.

So he shook his head and cut her off. "I know it's the concussion, but it's still my reality."

"I know it's tough." She stopped, forcing him to come to a halt, forcing him to face her. The compassion in her blue eyes almost undid him. "Time will help. It's really only been a few days."

"On top of everything else, I'm a billionaire and I live in a hotel. There's nowhere I can go, nothing I can do where I'm not recognized. And if that's not enough, I have an entourage standing by to critique my every move."

Invading his space, she cupped his face in her hands and read him. He stood still under her intense regard, but it took an effort. Finally she nodded and surprised him by brushing her soft lips across his cheek. He almost missed what she said next. "You need to give yourself a break."

She stepped back and swiped at his cheek where her lips had rested. "I'm sorry. I shouldn't have done that."

Suddenly he fought a minor battle between pulling his head away to keep her from brushing the kiss away and the desire to lean into her touch. "You can put your lips on me anytime you want. The professional standard is yours, not mine."

"And it's a good standard." With her hands on her hips, she seemed to waver, then set her chin. "Back to my point. You need to relax, not take everything so seriously. Remember, you chose not to tell anyone about your memory loss. If you want to change your mind, you can. People would understand."

"No." Because she'd opened the door to it, he leaned down and kissed her silky cheek, inhaling her clean, orange-blossom scent. The tension coiled deep in him eased a little more, allowing him to breathe freely. He linked his fingers with hers and started walking again. "The only thing worse than being stared at would be being stared at with pity."

"Compassion and empathy are not pity."

"Yes, they are."

"You could tell your royal guard. Much of their protective posturing was because they care about you."

"Maybe," he conceded. "They seem decent enough. But I'm still peeved at them for their treatment of you." He spied a boutique with evening wear in the window and veered in that direction. "I'd have to know them better first."

"You really don't need to worry over every little move, every little detail. Letting your staff believe we're involved was a brilliant move. What they don't attribute to your concussion, they'll attribute to your infatuation."

"Ah, about that—"

"Don't pretend you came up with the idea on the spur of the moment. You had it planned out before Clay and Jethro ever showed up."

He shrugged. He should have known she'd figure it out. "A romance allows us easy access to each other without anyone questioning it."

"You could have discussed it with me. Whoa." Grace caught sight of their destination, of bold colors and daring necklines of the dresses in the window and dug in her heels. "Not this place. It looks expensive. Let's try one of the department stores."

He tugged her forward. "I like this place. I can afford expensive."

"But I probably won't have occasion to wear the dress again. Just because you can afford expensive doesn't mean you should waste your money."

"Nothing spent on you is wasted." He pointed to a dress in the window. "The red would look stunning on you."

She bit her bottom lip as she studied the gown, her gaze slowly turning wistful.

"Let's see if they have your size." He drew her inside.

The place smelled nice, like a beautiful woman. It was well lit and spacious. Most of the merchandise was modeled by mannequins for a full three-dimensional effect. An older woman in a black suit came forward to greet them. She displayed no sign of recognizing him and he relaxed.

"Hello, I'm Eileen. What type of occasion are you shopping for?" she asked.

"We'll be attending the Hawke Foundation Gala for Displaced Youth," Grace responded.

"Oh, yes." Eileen nodded. "We've sold several gowns to people attending. It sounds like it'll be a lovely event. And for such a worthwhile cause. Wait, that's tomorrow." Her eyes went wide, but she smiled. "That just means we work harder."

"We want to see the red dress in the window." Jackson got down to business.

"I don't know, Jackson," Grace vacillated, "it's so extravagant. I don't think I could pull it off."

"My dear," Eileen enthused, "the dress would be striking with your dark hair and light skin. It just came in today, and I know it won't last long."

"Try it on," he urged Grace. The longing in her eyes told him what she wanted better than her mouth did.

There she went, chewing her lip again, but she gave in. "Okay, but let me look around. Maybe try on a few simpler dresses, too."

"Go ahead. I'll wait here." He dropped into a chair in a seating area set up in the middle of the store. Let her have some fun. If he had his way, they'd be leaving with the red dress. "Oh, Eileen, she's not to know the cost of anything."

CHAPTER ELEVEN

"I WANT TO APOLOGIZE for the third degree we put you through yesterday." Sierra said as she sipped her second cup of coffee. Behind her the Las Vegas strip dazzled the senses.

"I understand." Grace responded.

The two of them sat at the dining room table. The counter between the kitchen and dining room held a full breakfast buffet. The men had just left for a morning meeting and had taken Jackson with them.

He'd brushed them off completely yesterday. Mostly her fault. After they finished shopping, she decided he could use a break, so she directed him east to Hoover Dam. He relaxed on the drive. As she hoped, being in control of something—even a vehicle—bolstered his floundering confidence. When she suggested they take the tour, he jumped on the chance. He'd been as excited as a child, and as inquisitive. He'd loved it. He'd been in a much better place when he got home last night.

"It isn't personal." Sierra assured her.

"It's very personal," Grace corrected her. "But I get it. He's been away and the last gal he was seeing hurt him."

"She did, more than he knows."

"What do you mean?" Grace pushed her plate away and reached for the last of her coffee.

Sierra studied her for a moment obviously calculating how much she should share. "I don't know what to make of you." She confessed. "You're nothing like the women Jackson usually chooses. He likes tall, beautiful and dim."

"Really?" Surprise sent Grace's eyebrows rising. "I would think he'd get bored with dim rather quickly."

"Oh, he does," Sierra assured her. "But he says he wants to be able to relax when he's with a woman, not talk."

"Hmm." Grace decided she preferred her version of Jackson.

"Right?" Sierra demanded as if she'd been awaiting validation of her opinion. "Okay, dim is probably overstating it. And in all fairness, next to him most people fall short on the IQ range."

"Perhaps it's a form of self-defense for him. Maybe dim—for lack of a better word—equates with lack of calculation. So he feels he can trust their emotions more."

Sierra stared at her for a moment. "I never considered that, but you may well be right. Not that he gives his trust. He's the most guarded man I know. And the other three aren't far behind. I understand the foster care shuffle will do that to you."

"The four of them are lucky they found each other," Grace stated.

"Yes, they were all in the same house late in their teens. A good home run by an older couple known for taking on tough cases. They became a family. I met them in college, except Clay, who joined the marines. He joined them in the business later, after it was more established."

"I was a military brat," Grace told her. "So I know how hard it is to pack up and leave the familiar for the unknown. You learn not to expose yourself to the hurt of leaving friends behind by putting up guards."

"Yes. It's created a bond between them that won't be easily broken. But the wealth they've accumulated hasn't made relationships easy, especially for Jackson. Being a billionaire always raises the question of whether the woman is with him for the man or the money. His reticence is as much self-preservation as it is habit."

"But Vanessa got to him."

"Yes, and by hurting him physically she messed with his mind. Any emotional advancement he'd made in the past few years was shot to heck. He went off by himself while the police investigated and we didn't see him for weeks. We've been worried."

"It must have been traumatic. Some alone time is probably just what he needed."

"Obviously. He seems happy. I've never seen him be with anyone like he is with you. I really don't know what to make of it."

"And how is that?"

"Open. Accessible. He doesn't generally allow his companions in the penthouse. He has a suite on a lower floor he uses when he's keeping company."

Did he? Interesting. No wonder his inner circle was so freaked-out.

"I wouldn't make too much of it." Grace downplayed the importance for Sierra's sake. "We've been through a lot together the past few days.

When the novelty wears off, I'll be on my way and things will get back to normal."

Sierra wagged a finger at Grace. "That would make the guys happy. But I'm not so sure it would be for the best. I think you're good for Jackson."

"Hmm. And what about you? Who's the guy?"

"What do you mean?"

"You wouldn't be telling me all this if you didn't have romance on the mind. Who are you on the fence about?"

Flustered, Sierra tried to wave Grace off. "I'm not seeing anyone right now."

"But you want to." Grace prompted her. "Who is he, a coworker, friend of a friend? No, then they could champion him. Someone you met at an event?" Grace continued to guess. "Or through work?" Ah, a blush. "That's it. Not a coworker then, but maybe a vendor?"

"Okay, you got me." Sierra tried to hide a smile. Oh, yeah, she was in serious crush mode. "He works for the city. He's in charge of juvenile activities. We've been working together on the foundation gala. We've had coffee a couple of times. He seems really nice."

"And you're wondering if he's interested in you, your money or your connections?"

Eyes wistful Sierra nodded. "It's so hard to know when your emotions are engaged whether you're being played or not."

"So check him out," Grace suggested. "You have the resources. As I know from experience."

"I couldn't." Sierra got fidgety. "The reports we draw are pretty inclusive, because we deal in large amounts of money on business deals, and this is a highly competitive field so we want to be sure of who we're hiring. But this is personal. I don't want to violate his privacy in that way."

"So don't run a report. Do a social search." Grace got up to get her computer from the living room. She set it on the table and pulled up the biggest social media platform on the internet. "What's his name?"

"Oh, we can't do this." Sierra moved her chair closer. "We shouldn't do this, should we?"

"We should. A woman needs to be careful in this day and age. A man, too, as Jackson's experience shows."

Sierra gave the name Nick Collins. Grace typed it in.

"This takes patience," Grace explained as she clicked through pages, cut and pasted information.

Sierra leaned forward to read better. A few minutes later, Grace handed her a report that held public details of his career, community involvements and relationships. "It's by no means a comprehensive report, but you'll have a good sense of who he is."

"Obviously he has some issues." Disappointment filled Sierra's voice. "This was very helpful, Grace. You're easy to talk to." Sierra set her coffee cup aside. "No wonder Jackson and Ryan like you so much."

More than surprised by that, Grace had to smile. "Ryan likes me?"

"Oh, yes. You stood up to him. Presented your arguments as if you didn't care if he accepted them or not, and got Jackson to agree to Dr. Wilcox's examination without putting up a fight. Ryan was quite impressed."

"Really?" Surprising, but Grace would take it. If Ryan liked her, all the better for Jackson. This whole situation was hard enough on him. He deserved any break he could get.

"Really. And that's not easy to do. Well, I've wasted enough time on this." Sierra stood and gathered her dirty dishes. "I have to get to work.

Thanks for the help. If you're interested, I have friends who would pay for the same info."

"Sure. I'm happy to help."

Sierra nodded. "Let me know if you need anything."

"I will, thanks."

Sierra carried her dishes to the kitchen. "Don't worry about the cleanup," she advised. "I'll let housekeeping know we're done." With a final wave, she departed.

With time to kill, Grace decided to do another search. She went to her room and grabbed the file on Jackson. Doing the search for Sierra had given her some ideas for finding his father. Social services hadn't been able to find his mother's friend twenty-nine years ago. But times had changed. She typed in the friend's name and hit Enter.

Grace's phone rang. She pulled the cell phone out of her pocket but didn't recognize the number. She began to hit Ignore, but remembered she had job feelers out. This time with Jackson was only temporary.

"This is Grace Delaney."

"Hello, Grace Delaney, should I be congratulating you?"

"Doug!" Happy to hear her friend's voice, she sank down on the sofa and looked out over the Strip. "Why would you congratulate me? Did I get a job I don't know about?"

"Not unless you're ready to join the FBI," he responded.

"I've actually been giving it some thought. I've really enjoyed the profiling and background work I've been doing for Jackson. I might be interested in an analyst position with the FBI."

"We always need good analysts. I'll pass the word. But what I'm talking about is your upcoming wedding. The tabloids have announced you're engaged to Hawke."

"Seriously?" she asked, her heart clenched at the news. How she wished she could dismiss his revelation as sheer craziness. She and Jackson had known each other for only a week. But the truth was she'd fallen, and fallen hard. "Well, I can promise you any rumors of an engagement are greatly exaggerated."

"I'm glad to hear it," Doug said. "So how come I don't believe you?"

Because he knew her too well. "Maybe because I wished it was true?"

"You've fallen for him."

She nodded, though he couldn't see her. "Foolishly, I have."

"Why foolish? You'll make a great billionaire's wife."

Her heart squeezed even tighter. "Ah, that would require the billionaire to have feelings for me."

"So what's the problem? The man I saw clearly held you in high regard."

Hope bloomed, but she blocked it. She needed to be realistic. "I think you're confusing desperation for a connection. I was the only person he knew in a world gone crazy."

"I don't know. He was jealous of me. That points to a connection if you ask me."

"Jealous?" She forced a laugh. "You're imagining things."

"There must be something there, or the tabloids wouldn't have the two of you getting married."

"There's…chemistry."

"Ah." Silence beat down the line. "If you love him, you have to fight for him."

"Fight for who?" she demanded, raw emotion tearing through her. "Jackson has his name thanks to you, but his memories are still defunct. When he gets them back, I'll just be another memory."

"It's not like you to be a defeatist."

"No, I'm a realist." And an emotional mess. "He lives in hotels, Doug. And you heard me the other day. The only thing I'm certain of is a need for a home, for permanence."

"So get him to buy you a house. He's a bachelor, Grace. And travels a lot for business. Just because he doesn't have a home doesn't mean he doesn't long for one." A call sounded in the background. "Listen, Sherry needs me. Stay strong. The next time we talk, I hope I'll be offering congratulations for real."

"Give Sherry hugs from me. I'll think about what you said," she promised.

"I hope so, because you deserve to be happy. And I'm talking to Ken Case about that analyst position."

The line disconnected and Grace dropped her phone on the couch, staring unseeing out the picture window. Doug made it sound so simple. Fight for Jackson, get him to buy the home they both longed for. So perfect.

Yet so far out of reach.

* * *

Jackson sat at the head of the conference table, listening to the conversation flowing around him. He'd admitted to Grace to being nervous about reporting to work, but diving back into his life was both exhilarating and challenging. He found it fascinating, and luckily much of the knowledge was there, even if the details and people were still blanks.

Again and again he looked around for Grace, wanting to share something with her, but dragging his girlfriend into a meeting would be pushing it.

Other than that, the plan was going great. Her preparations, sourced onto his new cell phone, put all the pertinent info he needed at his fingertips. Names of department heads along with pictures, descriptions of his games, a list of ventures and properties he owned. No one questioned him looking at his phone.

It worried him sometimes that he'd become so dependent on her. Everything he'd learned since arriving in Las Vegas pointed to self-reliance. More, it was clear he kept women at a distance.

He couldn't imagine relegating Grace to her

own suite. The best part of his day was waking with her in his arms. But would he feel the same way when his old life caught up to his new one?

His past, losing his mother so young and being in nine foster homes before finding a home with Mama Harman, was a memory bomb waiting to explode. How could he know how he'd feel once those memories returned?

He couldn't. But he knew he wanted Grace by his side when that time came. She'd helped him through every mishap so far. He trusted her instincts, trusted her to put him first. Getting his memories back wasn't going to change that. No matter what those memories held.

The meeting wrapped up and Jackson met Grace in the lobby.

"Hi. Oh. Where are we going?" she demanded when he simply wrapped an arm around her waist and swept her along. "I thought we were going to go over the game plan for the gala tonight. I have the profiles for the invited VIPs. I also asked Sierra for a list of the coordinators and their assistants and did brief profiles on them. And I included the roster of your executives, with the pictures attached."

"Excellent. I can look at them in the car." A

large black SUV pulled up as he urged Grace through the door.

"It's going to take you a while to go through that." She slid in when he held the door open for her but stopped him from closing her in. "There are more than forty profiles for the VIPs alone."

"I'm good with facts and faces." He shut the door and rounded the vehicle. Inside the partition was up between them and the driver. "I will admit things seem to take forever to absorb. Took me nearly an hour to get through the file the FBI did on me when I was finally able to read it."

"An hour?" Her pretty blue eyes widened with amazement. "It took me all afternoon."

"I've found I'm a fast reader." He flipped through the file on the tablet she'd handed him, squinting, as his vision still blurred occasionally. That had been the only problem in the meeting earlier. It helped that she used a large font. These profiles included both personal and business details. "I'm amazed you were able to put this together so quickly."

"Yeah, well, I'm good with facts and faces, too." She gave him a rundown of her report. As the gala was a fund-raiser, she'd sorted the VIP profiles based on net worth. While he read, she fell silent as the wonders of the Strip caught her attention. Once they left the excitement behind, she turned to him. "Where did you say we're going?"

"To police headquarters. I made an appointment with the detective investigating my case."

"Are you sure you want to do this today? With the gala tonight? You're bound to see or hear something that makes your head hurt."

"Knowledge is worth the pain. We're here. And I want to get through this." He hopped out of the SUV. She was waiting on the other side. He took her hand and led the way inside to the information desk. "We're here to see Detective Hunt in Special Investigations," he told the clerk.

The woman directed them to the third floor and Jackson led Grace to the elevators.

She turned concerned eyes on him. "I'm just worried it'll ruin your mood for the gala tonight."

"And it may help me to remember." He pushed the up button. "You're always talking about my mind providing clues. Well, this is what my mind is prompting me to do."

"Okay." She squeezed his hand once they were inside the elevator. "But don't expect too much.

They probably won't be able to tell you much more than was in the report."

Her concern touched him. He bent and kissed her softly. "I'm glad I have you with me."

A bright sheen came into her eyes and for a heartbeat he thought she might cry. The very notion of his stalwart Grace in tears made his heart twist. But she smiled and the moment disappeared.

She started to say something when the elevator doors opened onto the second floor and a woman who looked to be in her fifties stepped on.

"Good morning," she greeted them with a smile and pushed Five.

From a distance he heard Grace respond. The woman's scent, an Oriental perfume with touches of citrus and rose, hit him the minute the doors opened. His head spun and pain exploded behind his eyes. He knew that perfume. From a long time ago. It belonged to someone important. Someone who represented warmth and comfort. He had the strongest desire to grab the woman and hold her close.

"Jackson." Grace pulled on his hand.

He didn't budge. The woman smiled kindly. "Jackson!"

He blinked at Grace. "What?"

"We're here." She drew him off the elevator. "Are you okay? You look like you just saw a ghost."

The doors closed behind him. He swung around but the woman was gone.

"Jackson, you're scaring me."

"I'm fine." He spotted a bench against the wall down the way and made his way to it. "Do you have one of my pain pills with you?"

"Yes." She sat next to him and dug in her purse. "Here." She presented him with a tiny white pill and a bottle of water. "What happened back there?"

"I did see a ghost. Or, more accurately, smelled one." Head reeling, he chased the pill with a sip of water and watched her brow furrow in confusion. "That woman's perfume struck a chord. I think my mother wore the same scent."

"Oh, Jackson." Her hand covered his knee. "What makes you associate it with your mother? Did you have an actual memory?"

"No. It was more like emotions that seemed to be from a long time ago. Sensations of love and warmth and happiness. But there was no memory, no face to go with the feelings."

His frustration with the lingering amnesia echoed between them.

"I think that's enough for today," she suggested again.

"No. Don't you get it? I need knowledge. If my brain won't provide me with the facts of my life, I'll get them any way I can." He surged to his feet. "Come on, we have an appointment."

He started down the hall but soon realized she wasn't with him. Turning around, he spotted her right where he left her. Arms crossed over her chest, she stood with her head cocked watching him. Damn it. He wanted her with him.

He retraced his steps. "Aren't you coming?"

Those watchful blue eyes never shifted from his face. "You've already had a traumatic event. I'll go with you, but only if I get to call a halt if it looks like it's getting to be too much for you."

"Yeah, all right." He grabbed her hand, determined not to leave her behind again.

Her hand moved but her feet didn't. When he came to a stop, he turned to glare at her down the length of their two arms. Her expression hadn't changed. "Promise me."

He gritted his teeth, disliking having limitations placed on him. But the one true thing he knew was Grace cared about him. It was the foundation of his world. "I promise."

She nodded. "Okay then, lead the way."

A few minutes later Detective Hunt stood to greet them. "Mr. Hawke, welcome back. And this must be Ms. Delaney."

"Please call me Grace. Thank you for seeing us on such short notice. I'm sure you can understand Mr. Hawke is anxious to get an update on the investigation. Do you have anything new on the assailant?"

"Not much." Hunt gestured behind them with the file in his hand. "Why don't we take this to a conference room?" A few feet down the hall, he opened a door and ushered them inside. "My partner is on a call regarding another case. She'll join us if she can."

Jackson nodded and sank into one of the cushioned seats. He reached for Grace's hand before giving Hunt his full attention. "What more have you learned about Vanessa? Tell me you are close to apprehending her."

Hunt opened the file, flipped through the pages. "Vanessa Miller's family has money. She gets a monthly allowance and all her household expenses are paid. She has no close friends. Interviews with her neighbors revealed she has a bad temper and sometimes gets violent. We got a search warrant for her home and found a prescription for an antianxiety medication. After talking to her doctor, we determined she has a psychotic explosive disorder."

"That doesn't sound good," Grace spoke up.

"No. People suffering from the disorder can be fine for long periods of time, and then something will set them off and they become verbally and physically abusive. It means she's capable of overreacting to the point of violence over any little thing. The medication is supposed to help, but she's known to go off it, which of course increases the chances of episodes. Your company has security on her residence 24/7, with instructions to contact us if she's spotted, but she hasn't returned to her home."

"You stated she has no friends or employers. What other avenues are you pursuing?" Jackson asked.

"We've interviewed the guests at the party where you met. Nobody particularly remembers her and nobody admits to inviting her. We talked to her neighbors. She's been involved in several disputes so we went out and spoke to the responding officers. Seems she is well-known for blowing up and then being very contrite. Always pays bigger and better for any repairs needed. Still, people are afraid of her and tend to give her a wide berth. She put her maid in the hospital for trying on a pair of shoes, but again she was really sorry, and the family paid the woman off, so no charges were ever filed."

The more Jackson heard, the angrier he got. "If she's such a menace, why hasn't she ever been charged or put in a care facility?"

"Unfortunately, it's not that easy," Grace said. "Unless she actually breaks a law there's nothing the police can do but take a report. Sometimes accumulative reports will build a history supporting action or adding to charges if any are ever brought."

Hunt nodded. "The family should do something, but they've set her up in the house and pretty much washed their hands of the situation."

"I am pressing charges," Jackson declared. "Someone who can lose their temper and stab a guy needs to be put away."

"I'm glad to hear it." Hunt shuffled the papers back together, and a picture slid out. Jackson automatically reached for it as he listened to Hunt.

"A lot of men are too embarrassed to admit a woman hurt them."

Forget that. "I think my reputation can survive it."

"Good, good. Have you remembered anything more you think can help us?"

Jackson exchanged glances with Grace. She gave a subtle nod that he took to mean she thought he should reveal his condition to the detective. He responded with a negative shake of his head. He couldn't see where confessing his vulnerability helped the situation.

"No, nothing new." He casually looked down at the picture. It wasn't the driver's license shot, which was what he'd seen before. This was a candid picture of a woman at a party. She had lighter hair, animated features and was dressed in a minidress sipping a martini.

Seeing her in the context in which they met triggered something in his mind.

He dropped the photo to grab his head as pain streaked from temple to temple and thunder pounded behind his eyes. He knew her. Vanessa, pretty, fun, crazy. Images, thoughts, memories began to crowd his mind, of her, of his past, his friends, his company. Everything.

It was too much. Too fast.

"Jackson?" Grace's voice sounded as if she was shouting in a tunnel.

"Mr. Hawke?" Hunt sounded the same.

"I'm okay." Jackson tried to say but it came out as a croak.

He wanted out of there. To be home. And alone until he sorted everything out.

Tension radiated off Jackson. That and the fact his grip nearly crushed her knuckles told Grace something was wrong. She hid her anxiety behind a polite smile.

"It's the concussion," she explained to Hunt. "He was in an accident a few days ago. Is it possible for us to have the room for a few minutes?"

"Of course, take your time. A last word of caution, Mr. Hawke. Vanessa knows she's done wrong. If she follows her pattern, she could be waiting for you to resurface in order to apologize. But she's clearly unstable. Do not engage with her. And your security people should notify us immediately if they see her."

"Thank you, Detective." Grace pulled her hand free to move to the door, a gesture meant to hurry the detective along. "We'll take every precaution. And I'll personally pass your message on to security."

"Tonight's gala is a public event. We're concerned she may take the opportunity to get close to Hawke."

"I'll have Sierra add you and your partner to the guest list."

"Thanks. Let me know if you folks need anything more, otherwise I'll see you tonight." Hunt gathered up his folder and left the room.

Grace closed the door behind him then rushed back to Jackson's side.

"Jackson, what is it? What's wrong?"

She got a groan in response. So not good.

She dug in her purse for another pain pill and the water bottle. The doctor had said Jackson could take two pills if necessary. He'd refused to take more than one and she'd practically had to force-feed the few he'd taken. But he gave her no argument about taking a second pill. He shoved it in his mouth and swallowed on a gulp of water.

Wanting to do something more, she began massaging his temples. He stiffened but didn't ask her to stop. After a bit she shifted her fingers to the top and then the back of his head, working down until she used her thumbs along the chords at the base of his head leading to his neck. He moaned and the tension lessened through his shoulders.

"You remembered something," she guessed. It's the only thing she could think of that could incapacitate him like this.

"I remembered everything." His voice was rough as if squeezed through a vise.

Everything?

"Congratulations." Joy for him washed through her along with a pinch of dread, but now wasn't the time for celebrating or anticipating the end. The surge of intel had obviously overloaded his senses. She needed to get him home so he could rest. His brain needed to shut down for a while in order to absorb everything. "Do you think you can move?"

"Yes. Just give me another minute." He reached for the bottle and drank it dry.

She used the time to call his driver and instruct him to meet them at the front doors.

Jackson pushed to his feet. He gave her a small smile as he reached for her hand. "If I fall, don't let them take me to the hospital."

"Someday you're going to have to tell me what that's about." Grace opened the door and they started down the hall. When he swayed, she wrapped her arm around his waist. His arm automatically went around her shoulders. "Lean on me. I'll get you out of here."

CHAPTER TWELVE

JACKSON LOOKED LIKE a billion dollars. The cut of his tux, the straight line of his posture, the jut of his chin, all spoke of confidence and determination, both elements Grace saw every time she looked at him. But there was more tonight. There was a surety of self that had been missing until now.

He was in his element, among his people. And he was thriving.

Still, she kept an eye on him, watching for any sign of distress or fatigue.

She'd tried to talk him out of attending the gala. He'd crashed this morning when they returned from meeting with the detective. Slept for hours. She woke him around four and suggested skipping the event or merely putting in a brief appearance.

He refused to hear of it. Said he was fine and proved it by pulling her with him into the grotto shower for a lovely interval. She'd been forced to agree he was fine indeed.

The memory brought a touch of heat to her cheeks.

Hard to believe making love with Jackson could get better. It had. The man knew his way around a woman's body. She had no doubt he'd made a thorough study of it at some point in the past.

He laughed at something said in the group he was speaking with and then wished them well and broke away. Several people had joined the group after he did, and she'd ended up standing somewhat behind him. Now she watched as he moved off without her toward the next group.

She slowly followed in his wake. He'd been solicitous all evening, keeping her within hands' reach. Until now. Maybe she should have been the one to beg off the event.

He stopped suddenly and swung around. A frown drew his dark brows together until he spotted her. The approval in his eyes as he walked back to her almost made up for his leaving her behind.

"There you are. I missed you."

She shook her finger at him. "You forgot me."

"A momentary blip. I'm told that can happen when you have a concussion."

"Oh, now it's convenient to have a concussion. I can't believe you're using it as an excuse to me."

"Hmm. Have I told you how beautiful you look tonight?"

Oh, how sly. Of course she knew he meant to distract her. And he knew just how to get to her. The dress was strapless in a deep true red, the fitted, drop-waist bodice hugged her curves to the hips, and the full ballroom skirt, completely covered in ribbon roses, flowed around her when she moved.

She'd never felt more like a woman, or more beautiful. Except in his arms.

Because she wasn't mad, just a little sad to see the end creeping up on her, she let him off the hook.

"You did." She swished the skirt back and forth and smiled up at him, enjoying the spark in his eyes as they lingered on her. "Thank you. For the dress and for insisting it was the right one. I'll never forget this night. I feel like Cinderella at the ball."

"Good grief, does that make me Prince Charming? I don't think I can live that one down."

"Not so." She straightened his already perfect bow tie. "JD may have stumbled a bit here, but Jackson is in his element. These people are lining up to eat out of your hand. You are every bit the prince of all you survey."

He glanced around at the crowd surrounding them. And there was just a little surprise in the gaze he turned back to her. "I suppose you're right." He wrapped an arm around her waist and pulled her to him. "I guess I'm just used to them versus me."

"I'm sure that's true in some cases." She leaned against him. "But not always. Tonight they're all backing you. This is a good thing you're doing here. And you don't need me hampering your progress. Why don't I find a quiet corner while you work the room for a while?"

Concern flashed into his green eyes. "Are you not feeling well?"

"I'm fine." It warmed her that his focus went to her first. "I just think you can move around easier without me tagging along."

"Absolutely not." He planted a soft kiss on her upraised mouth. "You saved my butt by interpreting Japanese for Mr. Watanabe. We were struggling without his interpreter."

"You were doing fine."

"I wasn't kidding when I said I missed you. My head is a mishmash of old and new. You help to ground me between the two. I can be myself with you."

It meant a lot that he felt that way. Love welled up causing her throat to tighten. She blinked back tears. Oh, yeah, the end was zinging at her with the speed of a bullet. But she could have this last night.

She cleared her throat and lifted onto her toes to kiss his cheek. "Okay, but if Cinderella's feet start to hurt, Prince Charming is going to carry her shoes."

"It's a deal." He kissed her again, lingering over the caress long enough to make her toes curl. Then he released her but kept hold of her hand as he headed toward another group of people.

He'd gone only a few steps when Clay intercepted them. "Jackson, I'll be shadowing you for a while."

"You've been shadowing me all night, Clay. What's changed?"

"A bit of a disturbance in the tunnel from the casino."

"What kind of disturbance?"

"Someone trying to break in. My men are handling it, and Hunt and his partner are headed over to check it out. It's probably nothing. But it means I'll be shadowing you from a foot away rather than ten."

"Do they think it's Vanessa?" Grace asked.

"Wouldn't that make the night a true success?" Clay fell into step with Jackson. "We should know soon."

"I can help if you need an extra hand," she offered.

"You're not going to need an extra hand, are you, Clay?" Jackson made it clear her assistance would not be tolerated.

"You do know I'm trained to handle situations like this."

"Yeah, I do. And I appreciate your willingness to help. But I won't risk you."

"That's just ridiculous." She tugged at her hand, wanting free of the bullheaded man.

"Don't care." He held on tight.

She threw up her free hand in frustration and looked to Clay for help.

He shrugged. "Works for me. I'm counting on you as a last line of defense."

"Ha." She smirked at Jackson.

He glared at Clay. "What the hell?"

Clay remained stoned-faced. "You're my number one concern. I'll use what tools I have to ensure your safety."

Jackson stepped right into her space and cupped her face, forcing her gaze to his. "How much would I have to pay you to get out of law enforcement?"

She blinked at him. What was he talking about? "It's what I do, who I am."

"You could learn something new with what I'm willing to pay. The thought of you getting hurt flays me."

The intensity in his expression shouted the truth of his words.

"I'm good at what I do," she reassured him. "And you were the one encouraging me to join the FBI."

"I was wrong. You should teach kindergarten or become a florist."

"A florist?" she repeated confused with where this was going. Seriously, she killed off cacti, something he didn't know about her, but still. She brushed the hair back at his temple. "Is your head hurting? Maybe we should take a break."

A pleading look toward the other man had him stepping forward.

"Jackson—"

"I don't need a break." Jackson ignored Clay. "I need for you to be safe."

"I am safe, right here by your side. You know as well as I do Clay isn't letting anyone get past him."

"And what about next week or a month from now? I have a scar to remind me things happen you never expect. Working in law enforcement comes with an expectation of being harmed in the line of duty."

"True. But I'm not taking money from you to change careers, so can we get back to enjoying the night?"

"Okay."

Yeah. He'd taken the hint in her tone and backed off.

"But the subject is not closed."

Or maybe not.

"I have confirmation," Clay broke in. "They just apprehended Vanessa."

Early the next morning, Grace woke to Jackson leaning over her. His lips caressed her cheek. "Sleep in. I have things to catch up on."

And then he was gone.

But there was no going back to sleep. Too much had happened yesterday for her mind to settle back into slumber. Not when she knew a difficult decision loomed ahead of her.

She was so happy for Jackson that Vanessa had been found and incarcerated. And still dread lay lead-heavy in her stomach.

His concern over her welfare touched her, but it also worried her. It would be different if they were a real couple, but her time with Jackson was more fantasy than reality. Their relationship was temporary at best.

She'd be a fool to let a fleeting lover influence her next career choice. Yet it would be too easy to do, considering she loved him. She'd known as soon as he regained his memory that her time with Jackson was limited, but with Vanessa still at large she'd figured she had a little extra time. Now that excuse was gone. She should make the break sooner rather than later.

Being a kept woman wasn't her style.

No, the fantasy only worked as long as she had something to bring to the relationship. Jackson no longer needed her, so it was time to go.

Just forming the thought in her head broke her heart. But it was for the best. She loved Jackson but not his transient lifestyle. She'd compromised in that regard for too long. She may be undecided with what she wanted to do for employment, but finding a place to put down roots was the one constant her soul never wavered on.

And for all his professions of missing her and his bargaining to find her a safer career, the longer the evening wore on, the more distant he became. Sure, he shackled her to his side, but he drew her into the conversation less and less. And for the past hour he sat her on a bar stool and completely ignored her while he talked to a group of old cronies several feet away.

It gave her a chance to observe him. He laughed, he talked, he listened, but always he maintained his distance. His stance, the angle of his head and the extra inches between him and those he conversed with shouted a need for space. And people gave it to him, happy just to have his attention.

His attention had been full-on when he made love to her last night, but his early disappearing act just confirmed he was reverting to his old ways. With each passing hour, the Jackson she knew morphed into the Jackson he used to be, which by all accounts meant a lack of emotional commitment.

What she'd learned from reading his file and talking with Sierra revealed a man shut off from the world. He lived in hotel suites, kept women and the world at a distance, and 90 percent of the work he did was in his head. His associates were his family, the company his home.

She couldn't live that way.

The man she knew wasn't quite so closed off, but with his memory back she had no doubt he'd soon revert to his former self. Too bad. The signs were there that he longed for more. He'd created the facsimile of a home by having all the penthouse suites designed the same. And his work with the foundation showed he had a heart.

He just wasn't willing to risk it by letting anyone too close.

So sad, because the man she knew was warm and generous, intelligent and funny. He'd make a great dad.

Good gracious, now she was thinking of children? That settled it. She threw back the covers and made her way to the bathroom for one last shower in her own personal grotto.

She needed to leave, and she needed to leave today. Before she completely lost her mind.

As Grace zipped up her duffel bag, a text sounded on her phone. Jackson, letting her know he was wrapping up a meeting and would be up in the next few minutes.

She blew out a breath. Showtime.

Carrying her bags into the living area, she set them down near the archway. Being a bright guy, Jackson was sure to get the meaning and start the conversation for her.

A few minutes stretched into twenty and then thirty. More to occupy her hands and mind than because she was hungry, she worked in the kitchen, putting together a snack tray of veggies, fruit and cheese. After a while, she heard Jackson come in.

"I'm in here," she called out.

"Sorry, that took longer than I anticipated. This looks good." A kiss landed on her cheek as he snagged a broccoli floret before opening the refrigerator for a bottle of water. "I've been thinking this morning. I've come up with the answer to your career decision."

A sinking feeling settled on top of the dread she already sported.

"I'm not going to work for you."

"Way to undermine a guy." His Adam's apple bobbed as he drank. "Why not? It's the perfect solution."

So not perfect. Silly her, she longed for a proposal, not a job offer.

To give herself a moment, she carried the tray to the living room and set it on the glass coffee table. Jackson followed on her heels.

"You can work with Clay on our internet security team. Electronic games are a highly competitive field. Espionage is rampant, but there's little chance of being physically hurt."

"Cyber security isn't really where my talents lie."

"You're being modest. I've seen your work, remember. The reports you've done for me, the profiles you put together for the gala have all been efficient and thorough. Top-notch." He reached for a piece of apple and spotted her luggage. His brows narrowed into a frown. "What's this?"

"I commandeered the suitcase you bought in Santa Rosa to hold the dresses you gave me. I didn't have the heart to squash them into the duffel bag."

"What are you doing, Grace? This sounds like goodbye."

"It is. You're home, Jackson. You have your memory back. You don't need me anymore." She thanked her years in the navy for managing to deliver the message in a strong voice.

A scowl drew his dark brows closer together. "That's not true. I have my memory back, but I'm still having headaches from the concussion."

"Dr. Wilcox can help you with those. And your friends will keep you from doing too much."

"Vanessa—"

"Has been apprehended. She's no longer a threat."

He cupped her cheek in his hand, ran his thumb over her chin, his touch nearly reverent. His eyes entreated her to stay. "I'm not ready to let you go."

Just for a moment she leaned into his hand, savoring the comfort of his touch, knowing this was the last connection they'd have.

"I don't want to go." The words squeezed past the lump in her throat. "Which is why I have to go now."

"That doesn't make sense."

"But it's the way it has to be."

"No," he argued, "there's another way. Come work for me."

Her head began shaking before he finished the sentence. "That's not a good idea."

"It's a great idea," he corrected, his voice going husky with his enthusiasm. "You're already working for me. You can just continue to do so. It's perfect."

"Except I don't want to work where a job has to be created for me. I want to be useful." Could he truly not see how he cut her each time he made the offer?

"You are useful. I couldn't have made it through the last week without you."

"But these were special circumstances. You don't need me to stand over your shoulder to do your business."

"Maybe I do." He broke away to pace. "Your notes saved me at my meeting yesterday. I've been vulnerable, not myself."

"Wrong." She wouldn't let him use his vulnerability against her, because he was so much stronger than his ailments. He'd proven that again and again. "You have been yourself. Pride, stubbornness, intelligence, determination, confidence—all those elements are you. The difference is your shields were down for a while. You've been more open to the world around you, allowed people to get closer. Experienced things like a regular man again."

"I'm not a regular man," he proclaimed with conviction. "I can't allow myself to be vulnerable."

That he believed that made her sad.

"Yes, you can. It takes a strong man to be open to being hurt. If nothing else, this experience has more than proven how strong you are. I hope that now you've regained your memory you'll take the lessons you learned this last week and apply them to your life going forward. Not all women are like Vanessa. They're not going to stab you. Give yourself a chance to be happy."

"Having you work for me will make me happy."

"Stop, Jackson." She couldn't take any more of this. His persistence chipped away at her determination. "Why are you doing this?"

"I told you, I'm not ready for you to go."

"Why not?" Her breath held in the back of her throat as she waited for his answer.

He struggled for words. And when he found them, they shattered her world. "Because I owe you."

She closed her eyes against the pain, then immediately opened them. Nothing to do about the fact they were overly bright. Forcing a smile, she began backing away, suddenly in full retreat.

"Wrong answer. Ah…huh." She cleared her throat. "But it's all good. An honest answer is never really wrong, is it?"

"Wait." He grabbed her hands and held on. "It is if it makes you leave. What did I do wrong?"

"For a smart man you can get some silly ideas. You don't owe me anything. I helped you because I wanted to, not for what I could get out of the experience."

"No." Shock rolled over his face. "I didn't mean that. You know I don't believe that. I want you to stay. We're good together."

"Oh, Jackson. We are good together, but we're nothing alike. I want roots, you want room service. I'm boots and jeans and you're a tuxedo and Italian leather. I need goals, schedules and order. You're spontaneous, creative and thrive in chaos. We are good together, too good. Which is why I can't stay. You think a few weeks together will allow you to work this attraction out of your system. But a few weeks together will only make it harder for me to go. Because it's more than chemistry for me. I love you."

He stopped his pursuit of her so suddenly he rocked on his heels. "Huh?" Wide-eyed, he stared at her, apparently stunned stupid.

Now there was the reaction a girl wanted when she revealed her love. Proof she was right to leave. Never again would she settle for less than love. And she wanted more than the emotion, she wanted the words and dedication that proclaimed she was valued above all else.

"Don't worry about it." She squeezed the words past the constriction in her throat, the pain in her heart. "My problem, not yours." Time to go. Her purse, she began a frantic search with her eyes. She needed her purse. "Listen, I want to thank you. This wasn't all one-sided. I learned a lot in the time we spent together." About herself, about a world she had no place in. "I met some really great people." She met his gaze straight on, because she wasn't a coward. "And a wonderful man."

She crossed to where he was still stuck in the middle of the room. "I've loved my time with you. I'll cherish it forever. Best it ends before it turns into something we both regret." She kissed him softly on the mouth. "Have a happy life."

"Sir," Jethro's assistant interrupted his meeting with Ryan, Clay and Sierra. "The manager of the hotel just called to say security has been dispatched to the owner's suite. There are sounds of destruction and breaking glass."

Clay's phone beeped as they all pushed to their feet. He met Jethro's gaze as they went through the door together. "Where's Hawke? He's alone? Are you sure? Where's Ms. Delaney?" The group stepped onto the executive elevator. "Okay, I'm on my way. Knock. If he doesn't answer, go in. If he's unhurt, I want you to pull back and wait for me."

"What's going on?" Jethro demanded. "Sounds like Jackson is trashing his suite."

"Where's Grace?" Sierra asked.

"She took a taxi to the airport twenty minutes ago."

"Okay, guys, that's not a coincidence."

"Come on, Sierra." Ryan shook his head. "It's not like Jackson to freak out over a woman."

"His relationship with Grace has been un-Jackson-like from the beginning."

"True," Jethro acknowledged as the elevator doors opened on the hallway outside Jackson's suite. Four security officers stood at the ready guarding the open door.

"Mr. Hawke is alone, sir," the head officer reported. "The room is trashed but he appears unharmed."

Clay nodded. "The four of you can go."

A crash came from inside the suite, followed by a foul curse.

"It's best if I go in alone," Jethro stated. The others nodded and he braved the threshold.

In the living room Jackson stood with hands on hips silhouetted against the Las Vegas skyline. Slices of fruits and vegetables were scattered at his feet amid shattered glass. Behind him the room looked as if a tornado had swept through—the coffee table was upended, furnishings were askew and the bar reeked of alcohol from broken bottles.

"You've made quite a mess here, buddy." Jethro joined Jackson at the window and, like him, stared out over the city. "Feel better?"

"No."

"Want to tell me what happened?"

"Grace left." Two words, devastating impact.

"I heard."

"I asked her to stay, to be with me."

"You proposed?"

Jackson heard the shock in Jethro's voice. Right. Why would he even go there? "No. I offered her a job."

"Oh."

"She said she loved me." The truth of that still rocked him.

"Ah."

He turned to stare at his friend's profile. "What does that mean?"

"Nothing. What did you say?"

Nothing. He'd frozen. Too surprised and confused by the declaration to act. Ever since he'd regained his memories, he felt out of sync, as if he was a round peg trying to fit in a square hole. He cherished what he had with Grace, but it was so far from who he was he didn't know how to reconcile JD with Jackson. Except to know he wasn't ready to let her go.

"She left. Why do the people I care about always leave?"

"At least you've known love, Jackson. My mom threw me in a dumpster."

That shocked Jackson from his fugue to focus on his friend. "Good Lord, Jethro, I never knew."

"Yeah, I don't share the fact my mom considered me trash very often. But for you I feel the need." He turned to face Jackson. "Not everyone leaves. Clay, Ryan and I are still here. You're my family, our family. We'll always have your back. The women in your life haven't left voluntarily. Your mom and Mama Harman died. And you knew when you started with Lilly how it would turn out. She was a year older than you, and there's no give in the foster world. Eighteen and you're out."

Jackson wanted to argue it hurt just the same, but his mother had loved him. He remembered her hugs, her laughter, how she had listened to him and read to him. Somehow he'd allowed the sadness of losing her to overshadow the love. The same with Mama Harman and Lilly.

But when placed against the stark knowledge of Jethro's experience he got some perspective. Maybe his recent experience allowed him to be more open to the truth. Grace's influence softened him, allowing him to trust again. He had been lucky to have love in his life. Still, the pattern was too entrenched in him to be easily shifted.

"Dude, you know I look on you as a brother. And you might be right about the rest, but Grace left." The admission cut deep.

"Did she?"

"She's not here, is she?"

"Jackson, Grace didn't leave you. She turned down a job offer."

"She knew I wanted her to stay."

"But did you give her a reason to stay? I've never seen you with anyone like you are with Grace. You've been different since you've been back. Happier. She's been good for you."

No denying that. From the moment he'd opened his eyes in a jail cell, alone and unknowing, to the long, duty-bound night of the gala when she'd stood by his side supporting and encouraging him. Her determination, intelligence and loyalty grounded him during a difficult time. Without her he'd have been lost.

Without her he would be lost.

"You're saying don't mess this up."

"That's what I'm saying."

"I'm going to need a plant."

* * *

The two-hour flight to San Francisco gave Grace plenty of time to suffer a few regrets. Pride sent her running, but had she flown from the only man she'd ever love? Shouldn't she have grabbed what time she could with him? He may not love her, but she knew he cared.

And that was the problem. Too often she'd accepted an inequitable relationship, even with her own father. This time she couldn't do it. She loved him too much to compromise. Respected herself too much to trade her pride for a few months' charade.

Doug had suggested Jackson might long for a home as much as she did, but the way he froze when she said she loved him shouted just the opposite.

No, she'd been smart to end it before her heart got more engaged.

Or so she thought until she walked into the garage at the San Francisco Pinnacle to find Jackson leaning against her SUV. Her traitorous heart rejoiced at the sight of him.

"What are you doing here?"

"I live in a tuxedo world, but I like jeans, too.

If you remember, that's what I was wearing when we met."

She blinked at him. "Seriously? That's what you want to say to me?"

"Yes. I run a billion-dollar organization." He blocked her when she tried to walk around him. "Believe me, I value organization as much as I do creativity."

"Jackson, this is futile."

"I'm not going to apologize for the room service. I'm sure you'll come to appreciate it."

"Doubtful, since we won't be together." She tried again to get around him, shutting her ears to his sensible arguments. She'd made up her mind. Again he blocked her.

"I'm not giving up on you, Grace."

"I'm sure there are any number of people able to play cyber cop for you."

He flinched. "I deserve that. But give a guy a break. I've had a lot to assimilate the last couple of days, and I'm told a concussion can cause confusion and disorientation."

"You keep throwing my words back at me." Why did he persist in doing this? She didn't know if she had the strength to say no a second time.

"What can I say? You're a smart woman."

"You're not making any points here."

The elevator dinged and a couple stepped out. They whispered to each other and laughed as they passed. It was a vivid reminder of everything Grace wanted. And Jackson didn't.

"I'm tired, Jackson. I really don't want to do this again." She deserved to be loved. Unless he had three little words to say, she didn't want to hear it.

"I could also point out that I don't trust easily, yet I invited you into my inner sanctum. I haven't done that in ten years."

She blinked again, the impact of his statement catching her unawares. She'd been so upset by the offer she hadn't seen it from his side, hadn't acknowledged the import of it. Still, nothing had changed. He'd offered her a job when she longed for so much more.

"Jackson—"

He placed a finger over her lips. "We agree we're good together. We can work out any differences, explore them, exploit them, rejoice in them."

"You're going to a lot of trouble to recruit a new employee."

"Forget the job." He leaned down and kissed her softly. "It's yours if you want it, but I'm talking a lifetime commitment. I need you in my life. The job was my way of keeping you with me. But I have a better way." Reaching behind him, he grabbed something off the hood of the SUV and presented it to her.

She stared at the plant, a charming little houseplant, some kind of ivy if she wasn't mistaken. "What's this?"

"The first plant for our new home." There was just the slightest shake to his voice. "I want to put down roots with you, Grace Delaney." No shake now. "In Las Vegas, or San Francisco if you want to pursue the position with the FBI. Wherever you want, as long as we're together."

"I think I'm going to start my own business as a private security consultant specializing in profiles and some private investigations. Including you, I've already had four clients. And I found your father."

"My father?" He looked perplexed, then

laughed. "That's wonderful." He framed her face. "You're wonderful. Will you marry me?"

This time she blinked back tears. The words were right, the gesture perfect. Dare she hope? For so long she'd believed home was associated with a person. It was how she grew up moving from base to base with her father. But as an adult that never proved true, so she thought she could find home in a place. With his words she realized home followed the heart, and she hadn't found it because she hadn't found the right man. Until Jackson.

But it would only work if he felt the same.

"Why?" she whispered, too afraid to hope.

"Oh, baby." He took the plant and set it aside before pulling her into his arms. He tilted her chin until their gazes met. "Because I was happier staying with you in an economy hotel and having no money than I've ever been as a billionaire. Because you get me. Because I trust you. But most of all, because I love you."

Joy burst through her. She threw her arms around his neck and kissed him with all the love in her heart. He immediately deepened the kiss with an urgency and passion that echoed her emotions. When he lifted his head, she grinned up at him.

"Right answer."

"Does that mean yes?"

"That means yes."

* * * * *

MILLS & BOON®
Large Print – December 2015

The Greek Demands His Heir
Lynne Graham

The Sinner's Marriage Redemption
Annie West

His Sicilian Cinderella
Carol Marinelli

Captivated by the Greek
Julia James

The Perfect Cazorla Wife
Michelle Smart

Claimed for His Duty
Tara Pammi

The Marakaios Baby
Kate Hewitt

Return of the Italian Tycoon
Jennifer Faye

His Unforgettable Fiancée
Teresa Carpenter

Hired by the Brooding Billionaire
Kandy Shepherd

A Will, a Wish...a Proposal
Jessica Gilmore

1115 Rom LP